I0654587

# Murder
# at
# Ravenswood Hall

## A Saga Preying On Oblivious Fools

*[Book 2: The Hap Pozner Series]*

# MJ Maccalupo

A story of despair, death and life beyond — well maybe?

ISBN-13: 978-0-9894340-6-5
ISBN-10: 0989434060

Published by Write Beyond, Wilmington, NC
Printed in the United States of America

Website: http://mjmaccalupo.com
Contact: michael@mjmaccalupo.com

# Acknowledgement

I would like to acknowledge the many 'characters' I have known throughout my life that have provided the fodder for this, my second novel. I would be remiss if I didn't acknowledge my family and friends who have provided the encouragement and impetus for me to complete this work. Without their support it might never have been finished.

I especially thank my wife, Gigi, who has been there to listen to every page over and over and over...; and for providing the needed criticism when something was just not good enough. Now that it is finished I can tell her, "You were right; thank you."

## Dedication

To the many people who have traveled through my life over the years and had an impact (many of whom never knowing it); especially Fr. Venard (Jerry Carr), OFM, my Spanish teacher at Bishop Timon H.S. in South Buffalo, who taught us not only Spanish, but to love life – and to live it. In his memory and in the joy that life has to offer each of us I dedicate this, my second novel, "Murder at Ravenswood Hall".

*Also by MJ Maccalupo* –

**"Where the Road Begins" (2011)**
*[Book 1: The Hap Pozner Series]*

# Part I: The Guests

A word of warning to all my guests;
They are revealing who know us best.
Beware your actions, safeguard your words –
Lest life's loose pleasures, gives flight to birds!

# 1

## Amiyah Dumas-Orwatt

**"A thousand injuries I have borne…"**
**Edgar Allen Poe**

"It was a cold and rainy night." No, that's been done.

"It was a dark and stormy night." No, that's been overdone.

"The night had a cool, damp mist settling in as darkness began to blanket the town." Now that's…

"Ada. ADA! For the love of God would you please get yourself dressed? Our guests are beginning to arrive."

My real name is Amiyah, but Daddy likes to call me by my middle name – Ada. He says it sounds more mature and sophisticated…whatever.

"Yes dear. I was just working on my new murder mystery and lost track of all time. Sorry. I'll be there in a jiffy." Arthur, or 'Daddy' as he likes to be called, has been really anxious about this dinner party. It's to celebrate his 70th birthday and we're having a few close friends over to celebrate with us; or should I say business associates of Daddy's – those are the only friends we have. I hate to say it, but I'm the one giving it and am really the least interested.

**"Murder at Ravenswood Hall" by Amiyah Dumas-Orwatt** will have to wait until tomorrow though. I must play the good hostess. After all he did bring me from a mediocre middle- class existence to the life of wealth and luxury, which is affording me the time and means to write my mystery novels – so...

"Davenport, would you be a dear and ask Clarissa to come help me pick out the right gown for tonight's party. I'm sure she's in the kitchen just sitting around bothering Mrs. Higgins. I didn't hire her to loaf."

"Why certainly, ma'am. I'll get right to it."

Having a butler, housekeeper and a cook is a world away from where I was raised; but, it's where I am now and I'm not going to blow it. Besides, I'm 25 years Daddy's junior and am sure to out-live him; especially with his poor health.

"Dear, I do apologize for getting so excited earlier. It's just that tonight's going to be more than just a birthday dinner party. You know how important it is for my business affairs, but I also have a big surprise for you. I've been dying to tell you, but I wanted it to be a special night for you as well. I have arranged for the guests to stay with us here at Ravenswood overnight due to the nature of the events that will take place."

"What! You know how I hate these kinds of last minute surprises. If you want to surprise me buy me a diamond necklace or a Ferrari; but overnight guests…"

"Wait until you hear what I have planned before you get yourself into a tizzy; and, don't worry, they won't actually be staying here at Ravenswood. They will be staying in other places around the coastal area. This will just be home base as it were."

"I just hope it will be better than the last time you came up with one of your hair-brained ideas when you almost…"

"Now Ada; let's not bring up old wounds. This time I have made sure everything will go as planned and everyone will have a good time; you'll see. I have been over all of the details a hundred times and I assure you nothing can go wrong."

"Aren't you going to say 'trust me'? Isn't that what everyone says just before the proverbial other shoe drops?"

"Oh, don't be so negative. This time it WILL be fun. You'll see…trust me."

That was what I was waiting to hear. He's so predictable. I could just kill him for all of his 'fun' adventures; but I won't. Little does he know that I found out all about what he had planned and have made arrangements for some interesting turn of events of my own for his 'adventure'.

"Now, as I was saying. After a scrumptious dinner that Mrs. Higgins has prepared for all of us, each guest and their spouse or partner will embark on a little adventure planned just for them. They will each go to their own specific location this

~ 4 ~

evening in and around the Wilmington area, where they will find packets containing instructions that will explain what their role is to be. In order to return here to Ravenswood they must carry out the instructions exactly as I have prepared them."

He paused to give me a smile and to read my expression, which he was so good at. He then continued, "Everyone will play the part of someone from Wilmington's haunted past – sinister or otherwise. At their location they will find costumes that they will wear as they play out the role they are given; and each location has been chosen specifically for the people and the role they play. The 'game' will end promptly at 6:00 a.m. tomorrow morning as those that remain alive will have the chance to tell of their adventure over a delicious breakfast in our home. And finally, I have arranged for…"

"WHAT! Stop right there. You had better explain that last part."

"Oh, I don't mean anyone will really be killed; it's all part of the game; it's a murder mystery. In fact, it involves several murders. Don't you see; for the past month you have been having trouble starting your new novel. I thought that I might be able to help you by creating this game and in doing so it might get your creative juices flowing once again."

I almost knocked Daddy to the floor as I leapt out of my chair and into his arms. Sometimes I feel as though I don't deserve someone who is so good to me; but only sometimes.

But just when I thought that he actually respected my work he had to ramble on and ruin it.

"Although, I must admit it serves a second purpose; this one is for me. This being my 70th birthday and all; well, I am feeling my mortality lately and decided to turn over a good bit of the power and control that I have to one of these, my top executives in my enterprises. As you are well aware, I have spent the last few months screening these candidates and this will be the final test to see who is best suited to take over much of the control of the company. This will afford me the leisure time to enjoy life with you more. Now doesn't that sound good to you?"

Just when I thought things were beginning to look up!

*    *    *

"Clarissa. Clarissa! Why is she always so slow? Sometimes I wonder why I even pay her."

"Yes ma'am?"

"Since you took so long in getting up here, I've already picked out my dinner dress. How does it look?"

"You look lovely, as usual, ma'am."

"Clarissa; would you be a dear and stay by the front entrance to greet our guests. I'll be along in a moment. You CAN tear yourself away from whatever important thing that you were doing, can't you?"

"Of course, ma'am. I'll certainly make it my job to greet YOUR guests with a smile and a warm welcome. Right away."

I don't like her snippy attitude toward me; and I try so hard to be nice to her – given her meager ability and intelligence.

As my father always said, 'there are some people you just can't be nice to'. Oh, well.

*     *     *

By the time I was ready Clarissa and Daddy had already welcomed most of the guests. I suppose it's a sign of a bad upbringing for me not to be there, but then again…

"Henry. Joanna. How nice it is to see you both. Clarissa, would you please show our guests to the study?"

I could sense a chill between Joanna and Clarissa. I realize she worked in Henry's home prior to and just after Joanna moved in with him. Joanna was the one who recommended her to me. At the time there appeared to be no problem between them; in fact, she gave her a glowing recommendation. And I couldn't agree more; or, at least at the time. She is young, strong and an extremely hard worker when she wants to be. But I could tell by Daddy's expression that he was a bit surprised by their body language as well. Mmm…

"Certainly. Right this way please. May I take your coats?"

"Well Clarissa, you seem to have made yourself quite at home here. How nice," Joanna said.

Henry quickly added, in a somewhat uncomfortable tone, "Yes. I hope you have found this to be a good fit for you."

~ 7 ~

I could see Clarissa shoot a look first at Joanna and then at Henry that spoke volumes. "Why yes, of course sir. I'm doing quite well, thank you."

As they left, our final guests arrived and made their grand entrance.

"Ada, Daddy; or should I address the soon to be famous author by her pen name – Amiyah Dumas-Orwatt," said Sunny, mispronouncing my name as **'am I a dumbass or what'** as she glided through the front door with her husband Brent.

"**Why yes you are** – welcome to our home and tonight's gala, that is," I said with a smile, playing on her bastardization of my name.

"So good of you to invite us to dinner tonight. We've been so looking forward to seeing you again. Why it must be ages since we have gotten together socially, and Brent and I have missed you both." Sunny chimed in without skipping a beat or showing her reaction – if she even got the dig.

What an actress! Well, at least Brent is part of the package, and he, on the other hand, is quite the looker. Sunny handles much of Daddy's business affairs for him, so I tolerate her; but I don't really trust either of them. I have warned Daddy many times that I think she has too much control over his finances; but he sees her as the strongest candidate to take on the new role – so far.

"Why Sunny, it has been much too long. Where does the time go?" Fortunately, I can be as phony as the next person when I want to be.

"And Brent, don't you look ever so handsome tonight. Why if I weren't married already I'd find you attractive." Another one of my left-handed compliments – and no one ever seems to get them. Oh, well.

Since the rest of the guests had already arrived and were comfortably seated in the parlor, with drinks in hand, I decided to put them all at ease.

"I know that you were all co-conspirators in this delicious deception. Daddy, just moments before you all arrived, told me about his sinister plan for the night and your complicity in it. And I want to thank you all for coming and taking part in it," I announced, as they all seemed to give a sigh of relief.

"You all know that in the past I have not been so keen on these kinds of things, but it really warms my heart to know that all of you are willing to help me with my book. And for that I promise to not only give each of you the first signed copies, but I am also going to make you a part of the book; that is, you all will be characters in it. Of course you know that some of you will have to die; but fortunately, it's only fiction; isn't it?" They have no idea of Daddy's plan for them; nor mine for that matter. Ha!

\*       \*       \*

Ravenswood Hall is a wonderful place. Oh, not as you might imagine a wealthy old man might live in; palatial, opulent and shameless. By mansion standards it is quite small and unpretentious; but it has history – which suites Daddy to a tee. It is really an old plantation home from the pre-Civil War era.

Ravenswood Hall was once the center point of Wilmington, an old southern town nestled along the southeastern coast of North Carolina just north of the mouth of the Cape Fear River. With its old world charm and sprawling acres it is a daily reminder of how life once was.

*     *     *

Being the gracious host (and not to be outdone by me) Daddy stood, raised his glass to our guests and announced, "I would like to take this time to thank all of you in advance for being such good sports by participating in this evening's game. I know for my part I look forward to what it will reveal. Before we begin I would like to toast all of you, and, of course, my beautiful wife Ada, who, without her little hobby, this adventure of ours would not have taken place."

That's exactly what he thinks of my writing – a 'little hobby'. As much as I appreciate the times he is kind and thoughtful, I loathe the rest when he is condescending and embarrasses me in front of everyone. As Montresor, one of Poe's characters once said, "A thousand injuries…I had borne as I best could, but when he ventured upon insult, I vowed revenge."

Just as I was about to melt into a puddle on the floor in front of God and everyone Joanna spoke up.

"Well I think that it is a wonderful avocation that Ada has chosen. I simply loved her first book and am anxious to dig into this new one. After all, she certainly has a talent for writing."

I could see her steal a glance my way and give me a hint of a smile saying 'we've got to stick together'. That made me sit up and hold my head high again.

But I knew where that was coming from and it wasn't necessarily any love for me. No, it was for her own sake that she chimed in. She had her own problems with Henry, her fiancé. He had his own way of subtly minimizing her aspirations in life. But why she stays with him when they aren't even married is beyond me. Granted he is good looking and wealthy, but she could do better. Then again, who am I to talk.

Joanna has a way of saying 'I've got your back' which translates to 'I'm turning the knife that I just put there'. Oh, I know she could say the same about me for all of the dirt that I shoveled on her over the past five years that we have been acquainted; but isn't that how life is?

Henry, on the other hand, despite his proclivity to put women down, has made his fortune (as have the others here tonight) off of the back of my husband, Daddy. Maybe that's why he likes to be called by that name.

"Yes, well then; let's move on to the dining room and begin our adventure with a wonderful feast. Being Friday, Mrs. Higgins has prepared a seafood dinner for you all to enjoy. Davenport, please tell our guests what is being served." Daddy was not to be outdone in his own house; and certainly not by an underling.

~ 11 ~

"We will begin with seafood bisque…" As Davenport went on, enumerating the list of items in the dinner, I drifted off getting flashes of ideas as to how the murder will take place.

# 2

# The Guests

"We, who are about to die, salute you."
- Gladiator salute to Caesar

I would be remiss if I didn't at least acknowledge the other Hapless players in this, soon to be, unfortunate adventure. As Daddy and I sit opposite each other at the two ends of the long antique mahogany table our guests are seated between us; the executives to his right and their partner to mine. Seated immediately to my left is Mariah, who (last I heard) was in charge of all day-to-day operations of Daddy's manufacturing plants. Every once in a while I accidently slip and call her Pariah, which is what she truly is. She doesn't find it the least bit amusing; nor does she realize that I do it with great malice of forethought.

Robert is sitting directly across from her. He is her ex, who she can't seem to get rid of; or maybe she just keeps him around for someone to abuse. While they no longer live together she seems to enjoy bringing him around to social events to demonstrate how cruel she can be. He's like a lost puppy that doesn't mind the beatings as long as he can be with the wealthy class. She affords him that opportunity, at a cost.

Don't get me wrong, I don't feel sorry for him. For his own part he is just as cunning and self-serving as she is. So I guess they really make the perfect couple, don't they.

Next to Mariah is Delmar, who is in charge of the HR department in all of Daddy's operations. Across from him is Alfonse, Delmar's significant other; a much younger man, who I believe is from Guatemala or some place like that – or at least that's what Delmar has told us. Of course, he also used to say that these young men were just his houseboys. How sad; he was afraid to tell us until now. I find Alfonse very interesting wherever he's from.

Delmar is a distinguished-looking black man in his late fifties who seems to always be dating young men from foreign countries; but he doesn't usually bring them to business affairs. He is afraid it would hurt his future aspirations; but Daddy insisted he bring him tonight. I found it refreshing to have a little diversity in our gathering.

Delmar is a jovial man who likes to tell jokes and laugh a lot. I don't know if that comes from an uneasiness about how others view his lifestyle, or if it comes from his fear of being caught with his hand in the cookie jar (so to speak); and believe me he is just as greed-driven as the rest. While he comes across as the least toxic of the group, I suspect he has a plan of his own of how to get some of Daddy's fortune, just as the others do.

Then there is Henry seated to the left of Delmar, with Joanna across from him. Henry has one of those obscure, but critical positions in Daddy's affairs. He deals with communications in the business; all kinds. Everything from press releases to charity benefits and advertising are under his control. I suppose it is a natural job for him to have since he is also a lawyer.

He sits only one seat away from Sunny in importance to Daddy. After all, the one who holds the purse strings must also hold the most power (according to Daddy). For my part, I see him as the best choice to take on the new leadership role that Daddy has in mind; but who listens to me.

And, of course, seated immediately to Daddy's right is his right-hand man (so to speak), Sunny. Brent is across from her.

"Well, aren't we a cozy bunch tonight; just like '10 Little Indians'. I hope you all get out of tonight's adventure everything that you deserve." I couldn't help myself. I had to throw that in.

"I think what Ada means is good luck to all of you and may we all experience success in what we are about to embark upon," added Daddy when he saw the reaction on their faces after my remark.

He had a way of manipulating things to his advantage in any situation. I guess that's why he's been so successful in business.

So there we were the 10 of us laughing and eating and enjoying the moment as if we were old friends.

~ 15 ~

But I know them all; I know them well. You see rank does have its privileges. That is, I know all of their dirty little secrets because Daddy (in a very real sense) owns them all. And since my "hobby" is writing mystery stories, who better to want to find out all about the people that surrounds her. Not to mention Daddy has the resources for me to find out anything I wish about anyone I wish.

"Ada, would you help me pass out the envelopes to our guests so that we may begin our adventure," Daddy said as he left the dinner table, encouraging the others to move along into the Great Room for the beginning of what was to be a very memorable evening for all.

"Why of course dear. I would be most happy to," I said trying not to let my demeanor reveal my pleasure knowing what is about to happen to them.

# 3

## Mariah and Robert

"O, wad some Power the giftie gie us
To see oursels as ithers see us!"
-Robert Burns
from "To A Louse"

"Robert, would you be a dear and put Daddy's birthday present in the car for me. I'm running late and must pick out the proper dress for tonight's party; and I still haven't packed my overnight bag. I have a feeling it is more than just a birthday party."

He can be so annoying sometimes. It's as if he can't make a move without me telling him; but I guess that's why I still keep him around. In a way, it's better than having a houseboy; he works for free...well almost.

"Mariah, there is something I would like to say. I know that you divorced me because of my job. I'm not you or those others you work with; I'm doing what I love and happy with my work. So, I don't make a lot of money, and you could say I lack ambition; but this is who I am. I love you and I know that some day you'll see that and we'll be married once again."

"Keep dreaming." He'll never get it, will he?

"I won't bother you about this again. Let's change the subject. How are things at work?"

"Daddy has seemed distracted lately at the office and I believe that it might have something to do with Ada. Anyway, I want to look my best. Oh, and while you're doing that, would you also be a dear and get my coat and put on some lights since we will be gone overnight. You can handle that alright, now can't you?'

"Of course I can." I could hear the restrained anger in his response; and I love it.

"Mariah, dear; I was hoping, that is, since we were taking this little trip overnight together, that maybe we could, well, you know..."

"Would you PLEASE get to the point instead of stumbling around for the right words. You know how I hate that."

Robert is such a mouse. I don't really care what he is thinking, but if he does find a pair and try to have an original thought he should have the courtesy to not waste my time having to bare the agony of listening to him drone on and never really get to the point.

"Well, I was just thinking that maybe we could share one room tonight instead of telling our hosts that we would prefer separate rooms. After all, we were once married and all of the other guests will be in their own rooms with their partners. I mean, if that wouldn't be asking too much. I could sleep on a chair or sofa in the room if you like…"

"Oh; alright. But don't think that this is opening any doors for you. You should be grateful that I am bringing you along for this party. And another thing…"

Out of nowhere, he interrupted me – I believe he has grown a pair. Well good for him; now I'll have to just clip them off again. I so do love doing that.

"I assure you that I won't take this to mean anything more than it is. After all, you did say that Daddy was looking at each of you for a big promotion; and this, I think, will make you look more stable – more settled and a better candidate than the others."

He was right about that. Daddy was a bit old-fashioned in many ways. He liked his people to be rooted and stable (as Robert put it).

"I suppose you're right." Oh, how it hurt to say that. "But remember, you are on the couch and this will only happen when it suits me."

"Of course dear, I wouldn't have it any other way." I could see the sweat break out on his forehead as these last words came out.

I think he began to feel a bit too courageous at his little victory, because the next words out of his mouth made me stop in my tracks and see red.

"I also wanted to talk to you about Brent. I know that you two…"

"You can stop right there! You don't know anything; and even if you did I am no longer married to you. You are lucky that I allow you to hang around. DO YOU UNDERSTAND!!!"

I don't know how he could have found out about the little affair that Brent and I have had going on for the past few months, but as long as Sunny doesn't find out, or worse yet, Daddy finding out, I see it as an asset that he knows. He'll never tell anyone, and it has the added advantage that he now knows his place.

Robert lowered his head and meekly responded, "I know that," and walked out to do my bidding.

Isn't life grand; and tonight is my chance to make the final move to the top. All I have to do is eliminate the competition; Sunny.

# 4

## Delmar & Alfonse

**"Anger is a brief madness."**
-Horace

"Alfonse, ALFONSE! For the love of Mike would you please get moving or you'll be left behind. I am not going to be late to my boss's party. I don't know why he insisted that I bring you; but he did, and you are not going to make me late. Now get packed."

"Oh, don't blow a gasket. I'm almost packed. It's hard picking out the right clothes for the party and for an overnight stay.

Anyway, if you weren't so insistent that I wear less flamboyant clothing it might have been an easier task for me. I suspect they all know what our relationship is so why is it necessary that I wear men's clothing to this affair anyway? You DID tell them; DIDN'T YOU! If not, then I'm simply not going. You can tell them I'm sick or…"

"And this is why I call you a drama queen. YES! I told them. They all know about you and me. There, are you happy? Now will you get ready so we can be on time?"

"I knew you loved me. I am not like all the others. See, even though you won't say it, you really care about me. Okay, I'll be ready uno momento mi amore."

"I said try to speak with an accent, don't try to speak the language!" It makes me crazy sometimes how he goes from down in the dumps to on top of the mountain within a matter of seconds; but, I guess that's also what I love about him.

Sometimes I could kill him, though; and if he ruins my chances at this opportunity I might. I am the best candidate out of all of us for this top position and I am not going to let Alfonse jeopardize that; after all, he can easily be replaced – I can't.

"And, just a reminder; you are to watch your drinking at this party. It is important that you keep yourself under control at all times. You know you have a tendency to over-drink. That could kill my chances of getting the promotion…and you as well. Remember that."

"And you call me the drama queen. Are you listening to yourself? The fact that I am invited should tell you that our relationship, your lifestyle, that is, has little to do with your opportunities. I'm looking forward to meeting this 'Daddy' person. He sounds just dee-vine. And I still don't see why I must wear these God-awful clothes. Where I come from men, and I mean real men, do wear silk and colorful clothing."

I just hope this little game we're going to play will keep Alfonse away from everyone else for at least a little while. Maybe I'll get lucky and can use him to distract Sunny. She's just as flamboyant as he is; they should get along wonderfully!

If I can get Daddy aside for only a few moments I can tell him about my idea for streamlining the human resource department and how important personnel are to the corporation. I know Sunny is pushing her own agenda, but if I can get him to see how important I am to the company and how I am the best one to lead the business I might just be able to eliminate Sunny from the picture. And once I am in control I'll eliminate her...for good. Ha!

"And one more thing; dear Alfonse..."

"Oh, here we go. Now you want me to do something unsavory to help you. Go ahead; what is it?"

"Now it is for the both of us – remember that. What I need you to do is to distract Sunny for a while. She is one of those self-professed liberal thinkers. You know; the ones that seem so interested in 'our kind'. In other words, she likes to be seen having a wonderful time with us, while looking down her nose at the same time."

"She, oddly enough, is a beer drinker; like you. Anyway, what I want you to do is engage her in a conversation about beers and that will give me time to be alone with Daddy for a while. And DON'T, whatever you do, DON'T say that dumb thing you say..."

"Are you referring to my speaking French? I shouldn't tell her that Daddy has a lot of – how you say? Gen-es-se beer."

"That's what I mean. Don't do it!"

"Mon dieu!"

"That's enough. Remember you are supposed to be from somewhere in the Caribbean…"

"Oh, really; where exactly might that be?"

"I don't care; pick a country! But for the next twenty- four hours you are earning your keep, understand?"

"Don't have a hissy. I'll do my part. After all, I will benefit as well. Remember, you promised to take me on a cruise once you get this new job."

"Yes, I remember. If things go the way I've planned, I'll throw in a new thumb ring as well. How about that?" "I want my birthstone – amethyst."

"Alright, alright; are you ready yet?"

"I'm at the door holding my bag…Men!"

# 5

## Henry and Joanna

"For all sad words of tongue and pen,
The saddest are these, 'it might have been'."
- John Greenleaf Whittier

"Henry. I'm home. I have the wonderful silk scarf we picked out for Daddy's present. Your clothier had it embroidered with Daddy's initials and gift wrapped it beautifully."

"I'm not interested in how it looks; I just want it to be the best gift he gets from anyone at the party. This is about positioning; and I MUST position myself to get that promotion. Right now Sunny thinks she has the edge; but I've got an ace in the hole that I will play if I need it."

"What is that? You know you're the best one for the job. You don't have to scheme and plot against everyone else to get it."

She does love me. She must to put up with some of my outbursts. I guess she is right, though; I am the best one for the job. Daddy's a very smart man; he must see that…but what if he doesn't. How can I get him to see things the way I do?

"That's easy for you to say. I'm the one who has to fight for the job, not you.

"Now Henry; there's no need to get angry and say things that I know you don't mean."

"Maybe I was a bit too harsh. I'm under a lot of strain right now with so much riding on this position. I'd feel a whole lot better if I knew that Daddy wasn't caught in Sunny's web. Now, Ada stands to take over the entire operation if anything were to happen to Daddy; and she favors me over all the others. She likes you as well; that is, more than she does the others. It's too bad she isn't more involved in the business; but I'm sure she has more influence over him than Sunny. And tonight will be the perfect opportunity to get her to help our cause."

"Here we go again; scheming!"

"I want you to have one of your friendly 'girl talks' with Ada tonight. See if you can get her to intercede for me with Daddy; you know, get her to see how I would be her best ally in the new position; and especially if anything were to happen to
Daddy."

"As for Daddy; I can take care of him…and I will."

My mind was racing; my juices were going. I knew what had to be done; and who had to do it. Tonight was my last chance to turn the tables. Sunny may have been the front-runner for this promotion, but Delmar and Mariah, no doubt, were hatching their own schemes to get in the front of the line as well.

~ 26 ~

I must not make any mistakes. To misquote Shakespeare, 'The game's the thing where I will catch the attention of the CEO'.

I hate to admit it, but Joanna might just be the bait I need to make it all work. Both Ada and Daddy find her somewhat charming and they do like me as well.

They both find Brent too much of a distraction for Sunny to ever take over such an important job; Delmar, while they don't care about his lifestyle choice, they find him too caught up in his personal follies to be an effective leader; and Mariah's lost puppy, Robert, is a joke to them – how you treat your partner is how you will treat your employees – and Daddy wants his workers treated well, all the way down the line.

# 6

## Sunny and Brent

> "Oh what a tangled web we weave,
> When first we practise to deceive!"
> -Sir Walter Scott

"If you only knew how naive you sound. It's a good thing you have me to take care of you. You'd slip and slide in your own shit if it weren't for me."

I could rip his tongue out when he talks to me that way; or better yet kill him slowly…maybe poison him little by little; and watch him get weaker and weaker until he needed me to keep him from 'slipping and sliding in his own feces – literally! Now that would be a treat.

"Now Brent; how many time must I repeat myself, you may be absolutely gorgeous and incredible in bed, but my dear, neither of those will last forever. And since I'm the only one in this room who works for a living I suspect it would be in your best interest to temper your passions or you might just find yourself replaced by a more reliable model. While I can afford a Ferrari, I still know how to drive a Chevy." I could see him cower at the thought of having to take care of himself.

"Now that that is settled, be a dear and put our bags in the car and warm it up for me. You know how I hate getting into a cold car."

He thinks I don't know about his trysts. I've seen the way he and Mariah slyly shoot glances and half smiles at one another when they think that fool Robert and I aren't looking. I don't have to see it to know; I can sense it. But I'm biding my time for the moment. I need things to be stable and calm until I am named the new president of Orwatt Enterprises. Then he can slowly fade from the picture...he won't be necessary and neither will she. And once Daddy is totally out of the picture (which I expect won't be that long) Henry and Delmar will be cleaning out their desks as well. It will be time to make a clean sweep of things. Then, of course, there's Ada; poor, dumb Ada. What will become of her? I guess I could leverage her out of the picture fairly easily; after all she's only a writer – and not much of one at that. Her business acumen ends with "I need some money to buy new clothes." She won't be hard to get rid of; but I'm getting ahead of myself.

"Brent. Are we ready yet? You know how I hate to be more than sociably late. We mustn't arrive before the others, or more than 15 minutes after the last of them do. Oh, and you are sure about the others' gifts? Ours must be the most opulent and grandiose. How are we to be superior if our gift doesn't reflect that we are?"

"Of course Sunny; I told you. I went myself to all of the others' usual stores and spoke directly with the managers. After a little financial enticement they even showed me the gifts the others purchased. Ours will certainly put theirs to shame. I suspect diamond cufflinks will not only literally outshine their gifts, they will cinch your getting this new position. Now if you're ready…"

"Oh, I almost forgot, I want you to spend some time with Mariah tonight. I need her out of the way so that I can get Daddy alone for a while and she will try to do the same. I hope you don't mind. I know what a bore she can be and how much you hate my asking you to do these awful jobs for me. But it would be ever so helpful. Do you mind?"

I can kill two birds with one stone. I know neither of them will be able to resist showing their hand if I just get them close together and alone. Once Daddy sees the two of them together, and how they just coo over each other; that will eliminate her chances of getting the job. And he'll see me as a martyr for having to bear this betrayal.

"I suppose it won't kill me."

…How wrong could you be!

"While you're busy with her I'll get Henry and Joanna sidetracked with Ada. How she loves to kibitz with the two of them; and all the better for me. Then my only competition for Daddy's attention will be Delmar."

"I'm not so sure you'll have to worry too much about him either. In my last spying job for you I was able to dig up some useful dirt about Delmar and his 'houseboy' Alfonse. It seems Alfonse has a bit of a drinking problem. I suppose you could say the drinking is not the problem; he does that quite nicely. It's the knowing when to stop that is. He's quite a lush I hear. And when he has too much he gets very vocal; about the two of them. He apparently knows a lot of secrets about Delmar that he is willing to sell for a few drinks. I'll make sure he is kept in alcohol until he crashes. Oh, and by the way, I hear his Caribbean Island accent disappears after he's had too many as well. It seems that's just a story Delmar spreads to make his living arrangements seem more exotic."

"Well. You do serve a purpose. How nice. Just be sure you do as I've told you…and look like you're enjoying it. Can you do that for me, sweetie?"

"Have I failed you yet?"

That nasty little smile ran across his face as he answered me. This might sound strange, but I could keep him around if it weren't for the lies, the deception. I don't really care that he cheats on me; and I don't even care that he's lazy and arrogant – those are some of his best qualities. It's the lies. I can't stand anyone who thinks that they are smarter than me and can deceive me. That I won't tolerate.

# Part II: The Quest

The game reveals our darkest fears;
It can be quite amusing.
But show yourself to rise above –
The lies of those accusing!

# 7

## The Adventure Begins

"Politics is perhaps the only profession for which no preparation is thought necessary."
-Robert Louis Stevenson


"So this becomes a game of politics. Who can rise above the fray and stand out as the leader of the group. Is that what this is about?"

My book is just a ruse for the others to fall for; another way Daddy controls the actions of others. It's always a game for him; it's always about winners and losers – and he must always be the winner.

"Well, Ada. I suppose that is one way of looking at it. I look at it as 'killing two birds with one stone'; metaphorically speaking of course."

As Daddy and I left the privacy of his office to rejoin the others I had to marvel at the genius of my plan – and no one suspects a thing; not even Daddy. Ha!

"I'm sure you are all anxious to get started. I trust you will all take this in fun and have a good time with our little adventure. As I mentioned earlier, each couple will retire to a location selected specifically for them where they will find instructions and costumes which they are to wear for the duration of our game. I must caution you though, that in carrying out the instructions you are careful not to bring harm to yourself or anyone else. Remember this is just a game. So, as they say, 'let the game begin!'"

As Daddy and I retired to the bar at the back corner of the room, allowing the others to commiserate as they read their assignments, I could hear some of the buzz going on around the room.

These were not naïve people; they are all cut-throat, savvy predators. I could hear them question if this was a test of who could beat the others to rise to the position of second in command of Orwatt Enterprises; and they were right.

"Well then, I trust you all have had enough time to review your assignments, as well as to compare them with that of the others. I do think, however, it would be stimulating for us all to hear where you will be going and what you might anticipate on your adventure."

~ 34 ~

Daddy always enjoyed seeing other people squirm. He also reveled in their anguish as they had to make predictions without too many facts to work with. I guess this was a good skill to have if you plan to lead a company – and Daddy had it. It was now up to them to show him that they possess the skill as well.

"Henry. What do you anticipate is in store for you and your bride-to-be, Joanna?" A demonic smile stole across Daddy's lips as he quizzed each of his subordinates. His starting with Henry had more to do with proximity than hierarchy; he had nudged Sunny over and was standing closest to him.

"Joanna and I are to go to Bald Head Island where we will find our costumes and instructions at the southern most tip of the island. I would imagine our adventure will involve a boat or a ship; possibly a shipwreck, given the waters around the Cape Fear."

Daddy's eyes lit up as he heard his remark, "We're off to a wonderful start. You don't know how right you are; but you will find out soon enough! Now Sunny; how about you and Brent? What do you suppose is in store for the two of you?"

This was his game; he was the master and everyone knew that they must play along. I think that Daddy was enjoying this more than the game to come. But little did he know what I had in store for them.

"We are off to a house in the Historic District of Wilmington. As I remember, many of the older homes were built prior to the Civil War and had underground prisons to hold slaves as well as tunnels that led to the Cape Fear River. Many of these have been only recently discovered. We are going to a house once owned by…"

"That's enough, thank you. I don't want to reveal the surprise you will have for the others upon your return tomorrow morning." Daddy loved surprises; especially when they were a surprise to someone other than himself.

"Delmar. Where will your adventure lead you and your guest?"

With a look of slight apprehension Delmar cleared his throat, wiped his now sweaty brow and began. He knew that if this was to be a test of which of them would emerge as the 'heir to the throne' then he must come across as confident and strong.

"Alfonse and I are off to Murrells Inlet, South Carolina for our part. I believe we will have the longest drive so I trust we will be on our way soon." Delmar, while a smart man, was prone to clumsy remarks like this.

I could see Daddy getting a bit edgy at this point so I interjected on Delmar's behalf.

"I'm sure that we are all anxious to begin our little adventure; but be assured that there will be ample time for all to arrive at their destination, complete the task put before them and to return back here in time for breakfast."

Delmar gave me a nod, thanking me for saving his ass on this one. I just smiled and moved on.

"Now Pariah; excuse me, Mariah. Whatever was I thinking? What does my husband have in store for you and Robert?"

She smiled at me with one of those smiles that say, "If only I could kill you and get away with it…"

"Robert and I will retire to a house located on Orange Street in Wilmington's Historic District."

I could see that Daddy had had enough of this as he abruptly ended the discussion, "Well thank you all once again. I see that it is now time to begin."

I couldn't help myself at this point. I had to add, "So be off, be safe and be sure to say your prayers that we all come out of this alive. Ha! You know, as the warning goes if you don't say your prayers – 'An' the Gobble-uns 'll git you Ef you Don't Watch Out!'"

I could see by the look on their faces that they were not looking forward to this at all. But play they must.

# 8

## Blackbeard & Drunken Jack

**"Fifteen men on the dead man's chest
Yo ho ho and a bottle of rum
Drink and the devil had done for the rest**

**Yo ho ho and a bottle of rum."
-Robert Lewis Stevenson
From "Treasure Island"**

"We not only have to play this stupid game to amuse Daddy, but we have to drive almost 90 miles to do it! I don't see any of the others driving all over God's creation, do you? Alfonse; Alfonse! I'm talking to you. Would you please pay attention; are you listening to me?"

"Of course I'm listening to you. I have to. You have me cooped up in this car with the windows up and the radio off; I have no choice but to listen to your ramblings. So what do you want me to say; I'm your captive audience."

"You could at least acknowledge my statement; even with a grunt or an 'ah ha', or some damn thing. We are stuck together for over an hour and a half, not to mention all night on some deserted island with only a pirate map to use to find our costumes and instructions."

I won't admit it, but Alfonse might have the right idea. We seem to get along much better when we don't talk; especially on long drives.

*     *     *

"Well. That wasn't too bad, now was it?"

"Delmar, do I need to bitch-slap you back into reality? You were the one about an hour or so ago that was complaining."

"Well, I'm just trying to make the most of it now. See; even I can have a change of attitude. Now it looks like that old row boat is for us. It has a small pirate flag sticking up off the stern."

"What's a stern? Speak English, would you." "It's the back, matey."

"Well e-x-c-u-se me. Why didn't you just say the back of the boat? Oh, I see. A little water and a leaky old boat and you all of a sudden become Captain Outrageous."

"Alright, alright; get in before it gets too dark to find our treasure."

"Okay Captain. I'm in the boat; now what?"

"Row!"

*    *    *

What a beautiful little island; pristine sand with a variety of shells, a few palm trees and a whole lot of sea grass and seaweed.

"Now, Alfonse, we follow the map to the buried treasure. Take that small shovel from the boat. I'm sure we're going to need it."

"Delmar, what is the name of this island?"

"According to the map it's called Drunken Jack Island. I wonder where it got that name?"

"I haven't a clue, but I could just see a cute little cabana over there; and maybe a tiki bar here – right at the ocean's edge. This may turn out to be a lovely evening after all."

"Now don't get too excited. Before you know it, you'll be wallpapering the palm trees."

"Ugh. Don't be so gauche."

"This way; let's go!"

It wasn't more than 30 yards over the dune that we found our spot. I had to dig because by this time Alfonse was too distracted by the 'beauty that surrounded him'. Fortunately, it was only a few feet into the sand when I heard the shovel hit something solid. There was a loud metal thump. And there it was; our treasure chest.

After we struggled to pull this beautifully antique-looking chest out of the sand and opened it we found a packet containing our instructions for the night. Also, there were two pirate costumes. Oddly enough they looked like they were made for us. Mine looked to be tailor-made for me, as Alfonse's did for him. Mine was obviously that of a pirate ship captain's, while Alfonse's was made to look like that of a crew member.

At the bottom of the chest, just below the outfits was what looked like some kind of jerky and other dried meat. But the best surprise was the several bottles of rum that lined the very bottom of the chest. Enough, I might say, for more than a one- night's stay for the two of us.

"I think it only fitting that we open a bottle and toast our host for providing us with so spirited a game tonight."

"Delmar, we shouldn't open the bottle until we have read the instructions and followed them. You never know; this might just be a test – or the rum might be poisoned, for God's sake!"

"That's what I like about you Alfonse. You always look at the bright side of things."

"If you're trying to be sarcastic, don't bother. It's not one of your strong suits, lovie."

"Oh; alright. Go ahead and read the instructions; but read fast, I'm thirsty."

"Well, isn't that out of character? You – Mr. Patience himself; can't wait. My heavens; however will the world keep spinning!"

"Okay. I got your point. Can we proceed, please?"

"Here goes."

\*    \*    \*

"A Warning to Blackbeard and his shipmate Jack:

Ye have but one night's fare to seal yur fate;
So drink and laugh and sing with yur mate.
The best of rum, the best of crew;
One will live, but one die too.

Build fires high, as night's chill numbs;
From mist and fog your ship's crew comes.
The spirits call, but heed the time;
They'll take you out to sea to die."

\*    \*    \*

I could see a puzzled expression build on his face as Alfonse read the little poem. He confirmed his confusion as he finished it.

"What for the love of Madonna does that mean?" he asked.

"I'm not quite sure; but it sounds like instructions along with a warning. Here let me see it. Yes. That's exactly it. All we have to do is to build several big fires around the island and drink the rum. The fires and the rum will keep us safe and warm for the night. I think we can manage that. We may have had to drive the farthest, but I have a feeling that this will be the easiest and most enjoyable part of the game for any of us."

"Yes. That's all well and good. You seem to have forgotten the 'One will live, but one die too' part," Alfonse said in a noticeably shaky voice.

"Right, it does seem to be a warning of sorts; but it is telling us that the spirits, I guess meaning the rum – you know, if we drink too much, as you have been known to do – the spirits will make us lose our bearings and go into the water and drown. So we must pay attention to the time and leave when day breaks in order to be back for breakfast. There. How was that?"

"Bravo, bravo. But I'm not sure about this whole thing. It's giving me the creeps."

"Don't worry. What could go wrong?" I said with very little confidence in this whole thing.

"Now you're beginning to scare me too."

I tried to move the conversation along, "Let's get into our outfits, build a couple of fires along the beach and open that rum I'm dying to taste."

"Please don't use that word."

"What word now?"

"You know – dying."

As we finished putting on our pirate garb, complete with real swords, daggers and muzzle-loader pistols we finally sat down to open our first, of what was to be many bottles of rum.

"It's odd how these costumes, weapons and even the rum bottles and chest seem to be from a time long past," Alfonse said in a low and quizzical tone.

~ 43 ~

"You're right. I hadn't really noticed that until you pointed it out. It is odd; but don't forget Daddy Orwatt can afford to make anything happen that he wants – even realistic props. So relax and drink up. We have another six hours before daylight."

I think it was perhaps around two in the morning that we were finishing the last of the bottles of rum and about to doze off in our drunken state when we heard a low, muffled noise coming from across the dune on the other side of this tiny island. The noise became louder as we both sat up and held our breath to see if we could make out what exactly it was.

Slowly we rose as quietly as possible and began to creep toward where this noise was emanating from. As we moved to the dune we could distinguish the noise as laughter and drunken men singing old songs of the sea.

In fear of being spotted we slowly and patiently took off our caps and lifted an eye to the top of the dune peering between sea grass blades for a glimpse at who or what was making all the ruckus.

To our astonishment and wonder what we saw sent a chill down our spines and sobered us up immediately. It was a band of pirates; some sitting and drinking around a fire; others dancing and singing as they waved their bottles of rum high in the air.

Before we could crawl away to our escape in the row boat we heard a voice from behind bellow at us.

"Ye be friend or foe? If ye be friend come drink by our side; if ye be foe stand and die where ye might!"

It was then that I realized that this must be part of the game. Daddy had hired these actors to come and play a part in our game. How wonderful! Leave it to him to think up such an amazing bit of entertainment for us. Alfonse had gotten me so worked up about the message that I had begun to believe that something bad would happen.

I shot a glance at Alfonse and gave him a wink of assurance that I had everything under control. I could see him breathe a sigh of relief. Then I responded.

"I am Edward Teach, and this be Jack my ship's mate. We're awaiting the return of our crew and ship to sail and plunder in far-away lands. We are friend."

"Well then; come join the crew and drink tonight. In the 'morrow we sail."

So we drank some more and sang and danced. Alfonse was having the time of his life. As it was well past the witching hour and I found myself in an unusually troubled mood. Alfonse had taken to one of the crew and they seemed to be having too good of a time for my liking. I don't know if it was the drink or the time of night, but my temperament went from hostile to explosive.

"Alfonse, what do you think you're doing?"

"Sir; I am Jack. I know no Alfonse. And as for my actions, they are my own and none of yours."

I became enraged at his insolence and backhanded him across the face. At this the whole camp went silent for a few seconds, turned toward us and then began to yell, laugh and taunt Alfonse and me.

The next thing to happen was beyond my belief. Alfonse pulled out his dagger and began to wave it at me as he laughed and staggered closer to me. As he lunged he lost his footing and fell toward me. I grabbed the hand that held the knife and swung it away from my chest. It turned in his hand as he fell on it. Then there was silence once more.

The man that he had been drinking and laughing with bent down and flung Alfonse's limp body over to see the long dagger embedded deep into the middle of his chest. He was dead!

All eyes moved from his bloody body to me. What was I to do? How did things turn so bad? Was this what Daddy had in mind when he planned this game?

"I didn't mean to kill him; I swear. He lunged at me, then fell on his own knife," was all that I could get out between sobs.

"I saw it. It was a fair fight," yelled several of the crew. "No.

He killed the young lad unfairly," others protested. "A trial; A

trial; we must go by the code!" came from

voices in the back.

The arguing and drinking continued as the men got louder and wilder. This was my chance to escape. So over the dune to the row boat I ran; but it was gone. Fearing for my life I jumped into the cold black water and began to swim back to the shore for all I was worth. When I came to the mainland I didn't look back, but ran to the car tearing off what pieces of the costume that I could as I went. Into the car and off I went without even a glance in any direction but toward Wilmington and Ravenswood.

By now what remained of the water and sweat were pouring down my face and throughout my being. My foot pressed the accelerator to the floor and never let up until I once again could see Ravenswood Hall in the near distance. It was only then that I felt safe.

But what do I tell them happened to Alfonse? How do I explain his death? Or do I even tell them about it? Was this part of the game?

*     *     *

Back in the main hall I was greeted by Ada, who seemed in a bit of a tizzy herself.

"What's wrong Ada? You look as if something is wrong."

"No. Well, I'm not sure. We can't seem to find Daddy. He left us about a half hour ago and didn't tell us where he was going. He seemed unusually distracted at the time. We haven't seen him since. But I guess I worry too much. He has been known to go off on one of his tangents. This might just be one of those. Anyway, how was your little adventure; and where is Alfonse?"

# 9

## James & Florie Maybrick

**"By the pricking of my thumbs, something wicked this way comes."**
**-William Shakespeare**
**from "Macbeth"**

"Oh Brent dear. Would you be so kind as to bring in the disinfectant wipes and clean a few things off in this musty old house. You know how I pick up the least little germ and suffer so."

"Of course Sunny. Isn't that my job?"

"Now don't be troublesome; just the things that we both know that I will need to touch. You can leave the rest of this old world charm just the way it is. After all, it's only for one night; in fact, not more than six or seven hours – thank God!"

The thought of having to stay in this God-awful place for more than a minute made me want to vomit. But, here we were. And if it weren't for Daddy's bidding I never would have been here. I know his thinking and I'm sure this is a test of some sort. Since I am the one everyone knows is going to get the new leadership role it's only a formality that I must go through.

I instructed Brent, "Now read our instruction letter again for me. It is supposed to lead us to our packet and costumes here in this old house."

\*　　　\*　　　\*

"On Water Street beside the docks,
You'll find a house with broken locks.
Inside you must to play this game,
In costume dress reveal your fame.

Once thought to be the Ripper true,
His wife, his knife, her venom too.
The man must leave to hunt his prey,
The wife concocting brew must stay.

Before the evening fun you see,
Once four, but now there's only three.
Which ones will pass this test tonight,
I leave that to the spirits to right."

\*　　　\*　　　\*

"I suppose we're in the right place. We are on Water Street at one of the Historic homes. The docks are visible to us.

The house looks abandoned and the locks are broken. So now let's search for the packet and costumes."

I was not enjoying this one bit and Brent could tell. He was trying to make the most of it, the dear.

*     *     *

"Sunny, I think I've found what we're looking for. Here in what appears to be the master bedroom on an old dressing table is an envelope addressed to Jack and Florie Maybrick. On the bed are two costumes laid out neatly. They appear to be our sizes exactly!"

"I'm coming up the stairs now. I just hope one of them doesn't decide to give out completely with all of the creaking they are doing."

As I entered the room I could see the clothing lying on the bed. Brent was right; they did appear to be made for us. They also were very stylish in an old world sort of way. They looked to be period costumes from the late 1800s.

We put them on and, for my part, I began to feel like I was living in the 1880s. A sense of Victorian elegance and simplicity began to overtake my modern world hardness. I spun around swirling my long flowing skirt across the hardwood floor, which somehow seemed to take on a shine and timber of a new floor.

Brent smiled as he stood erect in his fashionable grey suit with high button collar; pocket watch with fob hanging neatly from his vest pocket.

I sat at the dressing table about to open the envelope but chanced to glance into the beautiful carved oval mirror attached to it to see a young and beautiful woman staring back at me. I took the brush that lay on the table in front of me and began to softly sing as I ran it through my flowing auburn hair.

"How strange; I don't remember my hair being so long or quite this beautiful a color."

"My dear, you have always been this beautiful in my eyes. But I must say, it does seem odd that just donning this garb has brightened up not only us, but the room as well."

"The instructions; we almost forgot about them. I'll open them and read them aloud. Please have a seat and help me decipher them if you would."

A strange chill filled the room just then; as if someone entered to listen along with us.

\* \* \*

"Take heed dear Florie, but more so Jack:
If walls could talk these might scream out;
The tales of woe and death and doubt.
As Socrates once sipped this brew;
Give way to those that went 'fore you.

~ 51 ~

Jack or James the both may be;
But Florie brews the deadly tea.
Beware the drink, and hold the knife;
It's he that dies that has no wife!"

On journeys near to hunt your lust
Another comes to steal your trust.
As predator becomes the prey,
Beware to over-take your stay."

\*　　　\*　　　\*

"Now what in the world do you think that means?"

"Yes; exactly. Who are Jack or James and Florie Maybrick? What about the tea and knife? And who is it that is not married that will die? Jack, James or someone else?"

Both Brent and I were clueless. This snapped us back into reality. It no longer seemed a wonderful dream-world; it was becoming a nightmare.

"I suppose I could have looked up who these people are and the history of this house had I known we were going to be coming here. I suppose we could do it the old-fashioned way."

"Huh?"

He never did have a way with words…it's just a good thing I married him for his looks and charm and not his verbal skills. While I love to talk, I prefer men who listen or at least appear to be listening.

"You know; snoop around the house and look for clues."

"Oh right. I'll go back downstairs and see what I can find. You can stay up here and search the bedrooms. Okay?"

"You read my mind. Now get going."

*       *       *

"Sunny, I think I've found something down here. Come quickly."

"Yes dear, I'll be right there. You do remember you promised to get these rickety old stairs fixed, didn't you? I worry so that one of us may take a nasty fall and…well, you know. And why do you call me Sunny? Is that a new pet name you have for me? I prefer Florie, as you have always called me."

"Why…yes, of course…Florie. You're really getting into this game, aren't you? Now look here at this. Here's an old newspaper clipping about the Canonical Five; you know the five women killed by Jack the Ripper in London back in the 1880s. And here, here's a certificate framed and hanging in what appears to be an office naming James Maybrick as a respected citizen of Wilmington and member of the Cotton Exchange on the Cape Fear River. Now I get the connection…"

"Well of course dear. You are a very highly regarded member of this community and one of the finest cotton merchants between here and England. We all know that. But how many times must I ask you not to bring up those awful murders. It scares me and causes sleepless nights."

~ 53 ~

"Yes Florie. I understand that, but I think I know what our game is. Don't you see. James Maybrick was one of the men suspected of being Jack the Ripper; and his wife Florence, or Florie, was suspected of poisoning him by putting arsenic in his tea. In fact, she was tried, convicted and sent to prison for his murder. Some years later she was retried and set free. It's all right here in these clippings and notes.

"So those are the roles we are expected to play tonight.
But I'm not sure what exactly we're supposed to do; nor do I know who the unmarried man is that is supposed to die. And, while I'm totally confused, what his death has to do with you or me."

"Now dear, let's not worry about that. Let's have some tea and cakes before you must go out to your business meeting tonight. Shall we?"

"Business meeting? Sure okay. You seem to know more about this than I do. I'll play along. Let's retire to the study for our refreshments. Ladies first."

\*       \*       \*

"Thank you for a lovely cup of tea, and a wonderful cake. I'm sure I really have Daddy to thank for them. I'm off to my, err...business meeting now. I suppose I should just take a walk around the neighborhood. He probably has people planted here that will give me a clue as to what I'm supposed to do. Hopefully, I'll be back soon. In fact, I'm sure I will; I'm feeling a bit woozy. It's probably because it's so late and the sweets I just had; I'm not used to all this. It's almost 3:30 in the morning; only a few more hours and we'll be on our way back to Ravenswood. I'll be back shortly."

"Be careful love. I wouldn't want you to fall and hurt yourself. And please take this dagger. Keep it in your pocket; there are some unsavory characters about and I wouldn't want anything to happen to you, now would I?"

"Of course not; see you soon."

I watched as he left the porch and turned toward the downtown area and onto Orange Street.

\*      \*      \*

Feeling sleepy, I thought I would lie down for a few moments, but in reality it was more than an hour when I was suddenly awakened by the sound of two men arguing followed by a woman's terrifying scream. I quickly rose from the bed, put on my own clothes and ran to the front door. I flung it open and ran to the street. I could see a crowd begin to gather down Orange Street, at the curb in front of number 413. There, lying in a pool of his own blood, was my husband Brent – dead!

I must have fainted because the next thing I saw was the small crowd that had gathered slowly and quietly dispersing and disappearing into the morning mist. When I looked over from where I lay I could see Brent's lifeless body being dragged away by two people – a man and a woman; it was...Mariah and Robert!

~ 55 ~

# 10

## Theodosia Burr Alston
## & the Pirate Chieftain

"Had we but world enough, and time,
This coyness, lady, were no crime."
-Andrew Marvell
From "To his Coy Mistress"

"Henry, I think that this is kind of romantic. I hope the others have such an adventure to look forward to as we do. I only wish you were able to sail with me to Bald Head Island. But it is only a short journey and the crew looks competent. I guess the anticipation of our meeting on the island and the roles we play will be sort of exciting; you know, add a little spice to our relationship."

"I suppose you're right; but I just feel a little uneasy about you sailing in these waters at night like this. I should look at it in a more positive light as you do. Now don't forget you are supposed to be Theodosia Burr Alston, the daughter of Aaron Burr, the former Vice President of the United States and the wife of Joseph Alston, the Governor of South Carolina. My role is to be the pirate chieftain who captures you after your ship wrecks in the treacherous waters just off Bald Head Island. I suspect Daddy has already hired a crew of pirates to act as my men. We'll see how elaborate this whole thing is. I'll see you there; please be careful."

"Oh Henry; you worry far too much. I'll be fine. And maybe once you've captured me we can have a very romantic rest of the night alone. How would that be?"

"Joanna, there's plenty of time for that at home. Don't forget what hangs in the balance here. I'm up for the promotion to President of Orwatt Enterprises; and only Sunny stands in the way. Let's worry about getting rid of her first. Don't YOU become an obstacle in my way; or it'll be off with your head, matey! Har, har!" I had to throw that in; I hate to admit it – even to myself – but I won't let her screw up this opportunity for me.

"That's NOT funny; don't even kid like that!"

"Alright, alright; I'll play the game like a nice little pirate."

I wish I was on the boat. The drive from the boat dock, while short enough, was extremely boring. Just as I had predicted, when I arrived onto Bald Head Island, there they were a small group of men dressed as pirates waiting for their chieftain – me.

"Avast ye maties. We'll be awaiting any ship that runs afoul in this here rough sea."

I was already getting into the role. But as much as I was playing it up, the pirate crew seemed all the more real to me; in fact, it scared me a little at how much they really seemed like pirates of the early 1800s.

As we awaited the inevitable shipwreck and capture of Theodosia we ate and drank and told old pirate tales around the bonfire that they had already been feeding. I had this eerie feeling that I was no longer in control of the events taking place, and that what was about to happen had already been determined.

"Thar she be; caught on that shoal and sinking fast. To the boats men! We must loot her afore she goes down. Kill the crew and take any prisoners of value to us," was all I could hear above the roar of the sea as the men scurried to the old, wooden row boats and onto the sinking sailboat where Joanna was. This was all too real. I wanted out, but there was no way to stop it.

"There be a woman aboard, and by the looks, she should fetch a handsome ransom for us. Keep her alive; kill the rest!" I found myself empowered by the rush of the water and the screams of the men. A fierce fight ensued at the end of which my pirate crew had been victorious. The crew of the sailboat looked to be dead; it sent a chill throughout my body at how real this slaughter appeared to be.

There she was; radiant and stoic. Joanna no longer appeared to be herself. She seemed transformed – she was Theodosia. As she spoke I felt a calm come over me. I saw how she had taken up this new role so completely that I was assured that I was to do the same – so I did.

~ 58 ~

"Well, my lovely lady. You might be a prize worth a king's ransom. What be yur name lass?"

"Sir, I am Theodosia Burr Alston; the daughter of a Vice President and wife of a governor. I expect to be treated as such until I am rescued. Is that understood?" Her head held high and her shoulders back as she firmly gave this command to me and my men.

They say that the eyes are the window to the soul; and as I gazed into hers I saw the soul of another woman – not Joanna's. This was a strong woman, not the one that I lorded over. She was in command, not me.

"Yes yur grace! Ha, ha! Do you hear that men. Now bow before our queen." The men laughed and bowed in a mocking gesture toward Theodosia.

As the night advanced and the air turned colder we set up a make-shift tent for Theodosia with a small fire of her own nearby to keep her warm while me and my crew sat and drank some more around the main fire; all that is except for the three men that I had assigned to guard her.

As night approached day I awoke with a start as I heard men yelling and running around. I could see the three men that had been assigned to guard her bound and gagged. My first mate came over to me and said that they had fallen asleep on duty and the prisoner had escaped. For their crime, they would be beheaded as the code dictates. I played along, believing that this was all part of the adventure; but when the blades flew across their necks and their heads rolled onto the sand I knew that this was no longer just a game.

"NO!" was all that I could get out; but it was too late. Their lifeless bodies lay curled up in a mix of blood, sand and sea water. I sprang to my feet. I had to get away – I had to find Joanna!

As fast as I could, I ran across the island trying to escape these madmen and find my love. After what seemed like an hour I found myself exhausted and unable to run another step. I was soaked with sweat despite the cold early morning air. I fell to my knees gripping my stomach, which was cramped in severe pain from the wild run and all too much rum. It was then that I saw her; Joanna, or was it Theodosia. She was lying face down in the sand – lifeless. I crawled over to her, turned her gently over to see that the life of a young, beautiful woman was gone. In her eyes I could see the stare of that other woman; that cold, cruel reminder of what had happened long ago.

I turned from her and that's when it hit me; I began to vomit uncontrollably. In the distance I could hear the sound of men screaming wildly as they were closing in on me. These were my crew members coming for me. I, once again, sprang to my feet and ran; this time to the water's edge and into one of the row boats where I began to row for my life. I could see their torches lining the beach as I neared the mainland.

Before I was even at the shore's edge I dove into the water and began to swim the last hundred yards. I had made it; I was on the other shore. As I looked back the lights on the island began to fade into a mist as the sun rose over the distant horizon.

~ 60 ~

I threw off my pirate garb and, soaked to the skin, staggered to my car that awaited me just a few yards from where I stood. Into the driver's seat and off down the road I went; heading back to Ravenswood, staring off into the distance at the long and lonely road ahead.

# 11

## Ms. Wilcox and Her Suitor(s)

**"A coward is incapable of exhibiting love; it is the prerogative of the brave."**
-Mahatma Gandhi

"So now what Mariah? This big old house on the river, these Civil War costumes and I have the same role I do in the real world – I have to try to win you over. Maybe this time I WILL win."

"Don't get your hopes up; it's only a game – and, lucky for you, you DO have a chance. That is, according to what our instructions say. Now go put on that Confederate soldier's uniform; and maybe you'll look like a man for once."

"You do know how to make one feel needed. Maybe in your costume you'll not only be beautiful, but also genteel."

Robert still doesn't get it. After all this time he still thinks he has a chance to be more than my puppet. Oh well.

"Mariah; are you ready yet? Can I come in to see you in your costume?"

Captain Buford can be so impatient; but then again I can't blame him. I certainly have cast a powerful spell on him – and Major Newbern, my Yankee suitor as well!

"Why, Robert you can be so impertinent. You know that a southern lady must look presentable before she can be seen in public. I am almost ready. You can wait in the parlor, as any gentleman caller should. I'll be there directly."

"Yes, of course. Don't be long though."

*     *     *

"There. Now was it worth the wait? And you had better say yes; better yet, don't say anything at all." I could tell by his expression that I was a vision. His jaw dropped and his eyes lit up; just what I wanted.

"Mariah. You look incredible."

"Whatever do you mean? This is just something that I threw on. If I would have been given proper notice of your arrival I would have prepared properly. But, oh well...and what do you mean calling me Mariah. You know that you must call me Ms. Wilcox until we are officially engaged."

Oddly, it was at that moment I could see a change come over him. His gaze became a devilish smile; his posture that of a real soldier. Even his voice gained a strength that I've never known.

"My apologies, Ms. Wilcox; whatever came over me I don't know. You must forgive me as having succumbed to your beauty and lost all sense of respectability."

At this he rose, gave a bow, took my hand and gently kissed it. He waited for me to sit, and then he followed. We sat and chatted as if we were courting when a loud banging began at the front door. I took this to be part of the game, as nothing we discussed seemed to be going anywhere.

"If I may, I will dispel this rogue that dares intrude on you."

Robert, Captain Buford that is, got up and went to the door to see who was causing the ruckus. I stayed in my chair, still stunned by his sudden change.

From the parlor I could hear the shouting of two men – Captain Buford and Major Newbern!

"A Yankee spy; out of uniform and daring to call upon my love! Well, I'll show you your place."

"No. You don't understand. I'm here to…"

But, before he could finish I heard the door slam shut with the two men outside. A scuffle ensued and then I heard a loud thud. I ran to the door, opened it and saw Brent lying in a pool of his own blood on the sidewalk – a fatal wound caused by the bloody sword that Robert held in his hand. I screamed a blood-curdling scream.

As I stood there in disbelief I saw that a small crowd of men and women had appeared from out of nowhere and were silently standing over Brent's body. From around the corner I could see a woman running toward us. She appeared as a ghost at first, becoming whole as she got closer; it was Sunny. When she came to the edge of the sidewalk she suddenly stopped, put her hand to her mouth and fainted, falling onto a small patch of grass that lie behind her.

As quickly as they appeared the crowd seemed to disappear into the early morning mist. Overcome by these events, and in somewhat of a numb state I followed Robert's command and began to help him drag Brent's limp body off to the river. Sunny started to rise from the grass, when she saw us with Brent's body, and she once again passed out. When we returned to the house Sunny was nowhere to be found.

Robert and I made our way back into the house and, without speaking a word, changed into our own clothes, left the house, got into our car and drove off toward Ravenswood afraid to look back — or at each other.

# 12

## The Game Revealed

**"Good can exist without evil, whereas evil cannot exist without good."**
**Thomas Aquinas**

"I'm afraid this has not gone exactly to plan. We all have stories to tell about the night's events; and seeing that some of us are not present I think that we can dispense with formality and find out just what has transpired. I, for one, have my own mystery to unravel. But let's begin and don't leave a detail out," I said to the group that was now present.

"I'm still a bit shaken, but am happy to see that Joanna has returned safely. Oddly enough by the good fortune of having been given a ride from Delmar as he passed on his way back from Murrell's Inlet."

"And no thanks to you for leaving me on that God forsaken island! I could have died there…" Joanna retorted.

"I thought that YOU WERE DEAD! I don't understand what happened to me...or to you. The pirates, the ship; it was all too much. But let me begin at the beginning..."

As Henry related his tale the rest sat in a stupor, barely listening to him. I guess we all were perplexed by what we experienced.

"I was happy to find her alive. After what happened to Alfonse...I suppose we must call the police and let them know where the body is," Delmar chimed in.

Delmar related his story to us, ending with, "But I still don't know why..."

"Delmar, what are you talking about?"

From out of the shadows in the hallway came first a familiar voice, then a welcome face – Alfonse.

"You're alive!" Delmar exclaimed as he jumped up and rushed to Alfonse giving him a crushing hug.

"I thought that you were dead. I saw you lying there after I..."

"Well, guess again. I don't know what you're rambling on about."

I felt the need to interrupt, "Alfonse; tell us what happened to you."

"Well, after this brute insulted me and went on one of his tirades about my drinking I decided it was time for me to go and sleep it off. So I took the small boat and rowed back to the car. And, believe me that will be the last time I do so much physical labor. Anyway, I crawled onto the back seat of the car, pulled the blanket that was laying there over my head and fell fast asleep. The next thing I knew I was at Ravenswood, the sun was up, the birds were chirping and here I am. Voila!"

"But I saw you...I killed you...I don't understand..." Delmar had the same look that I could see on everyone's face.

Still in tears from what they presumed to be Brent's death Sunny and Mariah both stood to relate their tales.

Sunny shot a cold, almost evil, glance at Mariah who immediately sat back down to let Sunny tell her version of the night's events.

Next Mariah began her take on what had occurred. But as she began to speak we heard a faint clapping sound that grew as we heard each step of someone walking toward us through the back of the house. Through the doorway that leads from what was once the servants' entrance we heard another familiar voice – it was Brent.

"Touching, touching. I suppose I should be honored that my death should grieve so many; but, alas, I'm not dead. I'm right here. This is almost like being able to watch your own funeral. Not bad."

At his entrance Sunny stopped and turned toward him. When he had finished his little speech she addressed him with, "I saw you lying there – dead. How...what...?" She stammered a few words then became incoherent.

"After I left the old house that Sunny and I were at I was supposed to play the role of Jack the Ripper and wander the streets to find my victims. Instead I found myself lying in an alley barfing from whatever Sunny had put in the tea she gave me before I left. And, believe me it was not a fun evening for me. To add insult to injury, when I got back to the house at first light I found the house empty and Sunny and the car gone. So I hitchhiked back to Ravenswood. And here I am."

"Well, I guess 'alls well that ends well' as Shakespeare put it," added Delmar in his jovial fashion.

"Not quite so fast," I had to interject, putting a damper on his playful nature.

"There is one more person missing; and that is Daddy. He and I were not part of the game tonight. However, I'm not as concerned as you all were about your partners since Daddy has been known to go off into one of his offices here at Ravenswood to take care of some business concern. It does seem odd that he would do that when he knew you all should be arriving. Never- the-less he did want you all to know that this game was also the final test to determine who among you would be the new President of Orwatt Enterprises."

"Madame, I'm sorry to interrupt, but I think that you should come quickly and see something," Davenport stated.

It wasn't like Davenport to interrupt Daddy or me, especially when we were entertaining guests. This must have been something very important. So I followed him into the hall that led to the master suite. On the wall just outside the bedroom was what looked like a tic-tac-toe graph painted in red with letters in each box. Instead of the Xs and Os that you would normally see there were three letters repeated in each: a D, an O, and an A. It looked like this:

| D | O | A |
|---|---|---|
| A | O | D |
| D | O | A |

**Dad and Ada, Ada and Dad –
While one life seems taken, the rest will be had. As
blood flows like syrup; A.O.D. will be he – Before
day has broken, D.O.A. will he be!**

But what did it mean? As I stood there puzzled by this message, the others began to silently file in one by one to see what had happened.

"It's a message; a warning of some kind."

"Thanks a lot Sherlock. Of course it's a message," Brent shot back at Delmar's remark.

"It spells out something. It's not like a regular tic-tac-toe board. There across the top and across the bottom it spells out D.O.A. or **Dead On Arrival**. You know, like when a body is brought to the emergency room of a hospital and the person is already dead when it gets there."

"That's right Henry. But who is D.O.A.; Daddy?"

Tears began to run down my cheeks as Sunny speculated. For the first time I thought that I deeply loved him. It surprised me; I could see the others were surprised as well at this. In there minds the only reason I married him was for his money; and I suspect that Sunny and Mariah both were jealous that they didn't do it first!

"And what about that rhyme that follows? It appears to have clues in it. 'Dad and Ada, Ada and Dad'. We know that Daddy is missing, but Ada is with us here; safe," Delmar thought out loud.

"Look at the second line – 'While one life is taken, the rest will be had'. What do you suppose that means? If one life taken means Dad or Ada, then why does it say the rest and not the other?" Brent was on to something.

"The last two lines, 'As blood flows like syrup; A.O.D. will be he –Before day has broken, D.O.A. will he be!' make no sense at all. But I have a feeling that we had better decipher this message; and fast – before it IS too late!" I chimed in.

Everyone seemed to be in agreement with me on that.

"Maybe we ought to call the police. Let's go back into the library and decide what to do," Brent said as he seemed to take charge.

When we got into the library I overheard Brent say to Henry, "I don't think we should leave Ada alone for a second. From the looks of things Daddy might already be dead and she will be next."

As Brent moved away Henry exclaimed, "I think it is time to bring in the police."

With that Delmar, not to be outdone by the rest, grabbed the receiver and gently said, "Here, let me do it. You've had a rough night as it is."

"No. I think at this point it would be unwise to involve the police or any outside investigation. Daddy always hated unnecessary publicity, and this would bring too much attention to him and all of you. Let's see what we can find out first. We need to scour the house and grounds for him. If we don't find him, we'll call in the police. Agreed?"

I could see puzzled looks on everyone's face, but I knew I was right; this is the way Daddy would have handled it.

Suddenly, Henry spoke up again; I guess to make up for his previous faux pas, "I think that we should split up and search the house first. Someone should stay here with Ada, since her name was also on that warning as being D.O.A. Alfonse, would you and Robert stay here with her? And Brent would you go outside and look around the grounds? Sunny…"

"Just a minute Henry; I don't recall you being in charge here!" Sunny chimed in. She is not one to take orders from what she believes to be her subordinate.

"I think Henry has a good idea. Let's listen to him. What will it hurt to try this first?" I felt I had to come to his defense; I want him to win – and I am, after all, their boss; at least for now.

"As I was saying, Sunny would you be so kind as to check the out buildings and garages to see if he might be there? Delmar, check the basement level. Mariah, you search the second floor bedrooms and other areas up there. Joanna and I will check out the rooms on this floor."

"There, it's settled. If you would all please follow these instructions hopefully we will find Daddy. And please be careful.

If you see or hear anything, come back here and we will all concentrate on your discovery," I said, wishing to secure Henry's authority in their minds.

# 13

## D.O.A.

**"Five to one and one to five, no one here gets out alive..."**
**-Jim Morrison**
**'The Doors'**

They all dispersed, each to his or her assigned area. It wasn't too long after they left that we all heard a loud scream and the sound of someone running frantically through the house. It was Sunny!

"I found him. I found Daddy!"

Between her tears and incoherent babbling we could hardly tell what she was saying. We sat her down and gave her a small glass of Scotch to calm her nerves before asking her to relate what she had seen. By this time some of the others, having heard her screams, came running into the library where we sat waiting to hear what she had to say.

"I was in the garage where the limo is kept. As I was snooping around I saw what appeared to be a red substance on the ground just outside of the trunk. I wasn't sure, but it looked like it might be someone's blood. As I cautiously approached I tried to listen for any sounds of life inside the trunk of the car; but I heard nothing."

She paused to catch her breath and gave a painful sigh.

"Take your time. Give us every detail," Delmar spoke, trying to calm her.

"I took a deep breath and held it for fear of what I might find. I opened the trunk lid slowly and when it was fully up I saw him. It was Daddy; he was lying there lifeless with blood all over his shirt and some coming out of his mouth. He was staring right at me with a death look in his eyes. That's when I screamed. I slammed the trunk shut and ran back here."

With that she gave another brief sigh, fell back in her chair and drank the rest of what was left in her glass.

Mariah spoke up at this, "What are we waiting for; let's go to the garage and get him out of there."

"I think Delmar, Mariah and I should go. Let's leave Sunny and Ada here with Alfonse and Joanna. It has been all too much for them," Henry said in a commanding voice.
"No! I must go with you. He's my husband and I want to be there for him – alive or DEAD!"

They reluctantly agreed. Sunny, wishing to remain back, knew that she had to go; and so she did. Only Alfonse and Joanna remained in the library.

We left the room and headed to the garage. When we reached the main garage where the limo is kept we saw what seemed to us to be a curious sight; Bravo, Daddy's nine-month old Entley puppy was licking the floor just behind the trunk of the car – right where Sunny said she had seen blood earlier. There was no blood to be found on the floor or on the limo. As we formed a semi-circle around the trunk of the limo, Henry reached for the trunk handle and cautiously raised it.

We stood there for more than a few seconds in disbelief. The trunk was empty! Not even blood could be found inside. From the intensity of her scream we knew that Sunny couldn't be making this up, but where was Daddy – or his body for that matter?

"Are you sure you saw him here?" Mariah chided.

"Of course I did. Do you think I would make this up!" "Now, let's not get into an argument. I'm sure you saw what you say you did. Let's go back to the library and regroup," I said as I could see that they were all a bit edgy from this.

Once back in the library I spoke up once more, "I think we should resume our search. Please return to the areas that you were assigned. Sunny, why don't you stay here with Alfonse and me. Robert, would you be a dear and help Brent outside? The grounds are quite vast and I'm sure he would appreciate your help."

That was probably a bad idea, since I'm sure Robert suspected Brent's affair with Mariah; but the property was big enough that they didn't have to be anywhere near each other.

Not 10 minutes had passed since this ordeal when I heard a loud thud coming from directly below where the three of us sat in the library. I know that Sunny and Alfonse heard it as well as they both stopped and looked down at the floor.

"I think we'd better go see what that was. It sounded like it came from the room directly below us; that is the main servants' quarters."

At that the three of us sprang to our feet and raced down the stairs and down the hall to see Delmar passed out on the floor of the room.

After a few minutes of trying to bring him around he began to stir.

"Delmar, oh dear sweet Delmar; are you alright?" Alfonse said as he held him in one arm and rubbed his forehead with the other.

"It was him. I saw it. He was right there; up there – in the rafters. I know I saw it. Where did he go?" Delmar babbled.

"Who did you see? What do you mean up there in the rafters? Make some sense here, please!" was all I could get out.

"It was Daddy; he was hanging by a rope from that beam. I came into the room. It was dark so I lit that oil lamp. When I turned around there he was swinging from a rope tied around his neck. He was hanging there limp and lifeless. It was all too much for me. I guess I must have slipped on this damp stone floor, fell and was knocked out when my head hit it."

"Oh dear, you're bleeding. You must have hit your head hard when you fell. We heard it upstairs," I said as Alfonse had already taken out a handkerchief and was applying it to the wound on the back of Delmar's head.

~ 77 ~

By now Henry, who was with Joanna on the first floor searching, heard the commotion and made his way into the room to see what the stir was.

"There's something very fishy about this; first Sunny, and now Delmar. Either someone is playing a joke at our expense, or moving the body for each of us to discover for some strange reason," Henry said speculating.

"The answers must be in that rhyme. But what does it mean?" I interjected.

"Mariah, Brent and Robert are still looking. I'm going to go back with Joanna. I suggest the rest of you go back to the library upstairs. We'll join you shortly. Then we can plan our next move. It might be a good idea at that point to call the police. In the meantime see if you can figure out the message in the rhyme," Henry said in a commanding voice.

I could see a look of determination in his eyes as he spoke. He was not going to be out-foxed by whoever it was that was doing this.

"You'll all be safe together. I'll go first to check on Mariah on my way back to Joanna. Then we'll all join you in the library."

"I think we should follow Henry's suggestion," Delmar said with a sigh of relief. He was in no mood to be surprised again tonight.

*　　*　　*

It was quiet; much too quiet for what seemed like more than a half hour. Apparently, Henry had gone to the second floor to find Mariah and to make sure she was alright before going back to the first floor where he had left Joanna.

I convinced Robert, who had come back into the house with Brent, to go with me to find Mariah. It was then that we found our next victim. I say victim because we found her curled up like a ball, in the fetal position, on the floor just outside the master bath. We could hear the stir of the water as it poured into the old cast iron tub, overflowing onto the floor, just through the doorway from where she lay. Brent ran in and turned the water off as Robert and I went over to Mariah.

"Mariah, are you alright?" I said as I approached her.

"Yes. I suppose," was her only response.

She sat up as Robert lifted her head.

"There; in the bathtub. Face down in the water – Daddy."

I stood up and ran into the bath area only to find the tub empty, except for the water that hung precariously on its lip.

Robert and I helped Mariah down to be with the others where she sat, much like Sunny and Delmar, empty and lifeless from their ordeal.

We hadn't sat for a moment, nor had time to make sense of what Mariah was trying to tell us, when Joanna came running into the room and exclaimed, "Come quick! It's Daddy…"

# Part III: The Jest

Amidst the broken rubble;
Outside the faded dreams.
Lies hope and life and happiness –
Or so that's how it seems!

# 14

## Hap's Dilemma

**"An asp in the grass is an asp in the grass; but a grasp in the ass is a goose!"**
**-Slick**

"Hap, Hap, HAP! WOULD YOU PLEASE ANSWER ME!"

I hate it when she does that. I have got to finish this story; it's due in three days — 'Monday morning by noon or it won't be accepted' — as Professor Hartley pronounced yesterday. And I don't have an ending to my murder mystery. You would think I could get a little peace and quiet so I could finish it; but NO! Something else seems to be more important than my finishing my final senior project. My whole semester grade in this creative writing course, not to mention my graduation next week, depends on my getting this completed and turned in ON TIME!

There, I've rambled on and didn't get in trouble for it. It's nice being able to use my internal monologue to verbally blast someone without them even knowing it.

"Joanie, I've just got a few more chapters to complete; and it has to be done by Monday morning. Can whatever you need PLEASE wait?"

"I don't see how; you invited him, I didn't!"

"Oh, you mean Slick, don't you?" I snapped back into reality – one that I wished so much to avoid if possible.

Don't get me wrong; Slick's my friend, but he's been staying with us for over two months now…and he promised to find his own place when he got here from Buffalo.

"And, by the way, the only time our dear old friend gets off of the couch is to eat, go to the bathroom or sneak up behind me and play grab-ass with my butt. One of these times I'm gonna turn around and deck him; I mean it," Joanie snapped.

"Alright; I'll handle it," was all I could muster. I knew she was right. I did invite him to visit; but I didn't mean for him to move in with us.

"Susie came here after he did and she found a job, an apartment and hasn't been in our face every minute! Can't you PLEASE have Slick do the same…and I mean NOW!"

"Okay. Gees…why does everything with her have to be melodrama. I'm going, I'm going already."

As I left my 'Man-Cave'; my 'Fortress of Solitude'; okay, the little corner of the bedroom where I write I was trying to come up with a way to tell Slick he had to go. But nothing came to me.

I had invited him to Wilmington thinking he could get a job, get a place of his own, and we could be best buds again. Not move in with us, eat our food, sleep on our couch, and basically watch 'Rocky and Bullwinkle' and 'Road Runner' cartoons all day while we worked and went to UNC-W to finish our degrees.

"Slick; it's been over two months now…"

"Has it been that long?" he interrupted.

"Why it seems like only yesterday that I was helping you move from Buffalo to Charlotte, and then from Charlotte to Wilmington; or that I was trying to cheer you up after your father's death; or the time I…"

"I get your point!" You don't ever have to worry about forgetting anything he's done for you when he's around – he'll be sure to remind you; often. Then again how can you throw someone out whose always been there for you?

"Look Joanie is getting a little pissed at you grabbing her butt and saying that stupid thing you say every time, like it's supposed to amuse her."

"Oh, you mean 'An asp in the grass is an asp in the grass; but a grasp in the ass is a goose!'. What's the matter? Has she lost her sense of humor?"

"You see Slick, she and I are no longer just roommates; our relationship has, well you know, moved to the next level. And that requires that we have some alone time to see where it will take us. How can I put this…"

Okay, I get it. So you guys want me out of the way, right?" he said with a sullen voice as he crossed his arms and looked away.

"Well, I wouldn't put it so harshly; but yeh."

"It just so happens, while you two were so busy working and studying and writing your story I managed to get myself enrolled into the 'Marine Biology' program at Cape Fear Tech – AND, I got a part-time job at Robert's Grocery on Wrightsville Beach stocking shelves."

He paused a moment to catch his breath and then continued his rant, "Oh, and it just so happens – and I hate to break it to you; I will no longer be sleeping on your very uncomfortable couch or having to strain my eyes looking at that matchbox you call a television – I am moving in with Devon today. As you are well aware, he and I have been hanging around quite a bit lately and have hit it off – not the way you think; we're just friends. He has a two-bedroom apartment and a spare television that I can put in my room – which is perfect for me. So don't feel bad about kicking out your best friend in life. I can take care of myself," he said with a grin. That's when I knew it was going to be okay with us.

I thought I'd throw in a quip since the tension was broken.

"Slick, ya know why I like you?"

"No."

"Me neither!"

I gave him a smile and shook my head. He just laughed.

As it turns out, this was more of a symbiotic relationship than Devon just trying to do me a favor. Slick needed a place to stay and Devon needed someone to help with his rent.

"That's great! Look it, you're not mad – are you?" I didn't want any hard feelings. Slick had been my friend for far too many years. And we have gone through too much together for anything to split us.

"Nah, it's water up a duck's ass."

Somehow I had missed those 'Slickisms'.

# 15

## The Clock is Ticking

**"As Sarge always says, 'If it looks like a duck, and it quacks like a duck
– make Chanina!'"**
-Slick

"Hap, Hap, HAP!"

"What is it now? I'll never get this thing done on time if everyone keeps interrupting me! And by the way, don't you have to study? You've got exams coming next week, or don't people in the medical technology field study? Is that why medicine is so screwed up – you guys just guess? Oh, I forgot, you're just naturally smart; you don't have to study."

"No, I do study; but I have to say I'm a bit more disciplined than someone else I know. I get my studying done before things become due."

"Yeh, I guess being creative takes a little more time." "Well anyway, I thought that you might just want to
come out here and talk with your friends. I think that they have

something in mind that will help you finish your story. It's Devon, Marie, Brad, Susie and, of course, Slick."

I have to admit it; I was glad that Susie came down here looking for a job. I kind of missed her – especially after Slick came here to live with us. Now it can be more like old times. Unlike Slick, she only stayed with us a couple of nights and then got her own place – and a job!

As I left my desk to follow her downstairs and into the living room where our friends were all sitting I began to mumble to myself, "I'm never going to finish. My whole life is going up in flames here and no one seems to care."

"What are you rambling about?" Joanie caught the tail end of my little tirade.

"Nothing – nothing at all! I'm just watching my life flash before me. That's all."

"Stop mumbling and get out here. Your friends are here to see you."

"I'm coming."

Maybe I should just ask Slick to come up with a good lie for me to tell Professor Hartley. That's always been his forte!

"Well, have you come to watch me go down in flames? Or are you here to see if you can get a good deal on one unused graduation cap and gown?"

"Hap, be of good cheer. The Three Musketeers are here to your rescue!"

"Slick, there are four of you; and nothing can save me now. But thanks for the thought."

"Hap; there WERE four Musketeers. Don't forget about D'Artagnan – that's me, of course," Slick was quick to remind me.

"Well, I'm glad to see you remembered something of what you learned those many, many years in high school," I added.

"As Sarge always says, 'If it walks like a duck, and it quacks like a duck – make Chanina!'"

That caught Brent's attention since his father was from Poland and had escaped with his family shortly after the Nazis rolled in and took it over.

"Who is Sarge and how does he know what Chanina is?" he questioned.

"Oh, he's my dad; he likes to be called Sarge. Even my mom calls him that. He told me he had it during the war," Slick shot back.

"Wait a minute," I interrupted. I couldn't let this one go.

"Sarge never left Ft. Dix, New Jersey during World War II. So where did he eat this delicacy?" I had to push him.

"There were people from Eastern Europe that came over here, you know. He was dating a girl whose family came to New Jersey from Poland. And you know how Sarge likes a good meal – especially when it's free!"

We all had to laugh at that one; even those who didn't know Sarge. They knew Slick well enough to know that 'the nut hadn't fallen very far from the tree'.

"If we can get to the point of this little meeting of ours please," interrupted Devon. "Brad tell Hap what we got."

"Now, the way I see it is: **one** – you have a story due Monday at noon, that's three days from now; **two** – if it's late, it won't be accepted; and **three** – you haven't finished it yet because you're stuck on the ending. Is that where we stand?"

Brad was always counting things down and listing. I guess that's why he became a math major in college. He'll probably make a good accountant someday.

He continued, "So all you have to do; WE that is. All WE have to do is come up with an ending to your story. And since we've had to listen to it over and over and over...sorry, I got carried away. Where was I? Oh yeh, all we have to do is give you a good ending to your story. And I think Devon has come up with a great idea to help you figure it out. Tell him."

"Thanks for that long and oh so enlightening introduction. I feel like I'm on stage now. **Look it**...(*he stopped himself, rolled his eyes saying*) now you've even got me speaking Buffalo-ese! (*After regaining his composure he went on*) As I was saying, we've all heard the story, and we think it's really good. The ending needs to be a logical progression from the details of the story, right? But – it needs to have some sort of twist that, even though the reader is following the characters and the plot, etc. they are being misdirected so that the ending comes as a complete surprise to them."

"Great. So far you've been a big help. Now I know what I don't know; and still don't know how to end it."

Not so easily defeated Slick butted in, "Hap, don't you get it? We're going to become the characters in the story and let it play out for you to figure out how it ends!"

"Didn't someone once say, 'somehow Slick you always make the ridiculous seem absurd!" I had to remind him.

"Yeh. I believe it was your lovely partner there, Joanie," he said with a smile.

Devon jumped in again seeing how the four of us (the original Musketeers) were slipping out of reality and into the nostalgic past, "I hate to break up this little trip down memory lane, but the clock is ticking and we ain't getting nowhere fast."

"Sorry. Well, if you all want to help me how can I say no? No matter how good or bad this turns out I do want to thank you all for trying. Alright, 'let the game begin!'"

"Now the way I figure it is we need to start with the characters back at Ravenswood Hall finding the clues and searching for Daddy. Since we don't have a full cast some of us will have to play more than one part. Okay? Brad you play the roles of Brent and Ada. This will give you a chance to get in touch with your feminine side."

"You're a load of laughs," Brad said as he folded his arms and pursed his lips to play an angry Ada.

"Marie, you'll be Mariah. Slick you can be Robert and Alfonse. This will give you a chance to get in touch with…well, anyway. Susie you can be Sunny; somehow I get the feeling that the two of you were made for each other. I'll be Delmar – since

I'm already black, it won't be a stretch for me to play a black man."

"A GAY black man, that is. Not a stretch at all. Ha, ha!" Slick chimed in.

"Enough of the editorializing; let's get on with it." I had had about enough of the foolish chatter and was actually looking forward to this game.

"And of course Hap you and Joanie will be Henry and Joanna."

"Excuse me, but haven't you forgotten some people. What about Daddy, Davenport, Mrs. Higgins and Clarissa?" "Good point; but I figure they are not part of the group who are trying to figure out the clues; nor are they on the search for Daddy. So we can put them aside...for now."

"Okay. Even though it is my story I'll go along with it; but I think, at some point, we'll need to bring them back into it."

"Alright, is everyone agreed? Now let's get on our way to Ravenswood."

"Devon, you forgot one important point," I hated to burst his bubble.

"What is that 'oh great storyteller'?"

"There is no Ravenswood Hall! I made that up."

"Right; well, that does put a little kink in our plan, now doesn't it...mmm?"

"Hey, I've got the perfect place to use as Ravenswood; and it's not far from here. How about Poplar Grove Plantation?" added Marie.

"Great idea, but do you think that they will let us use the place?" Brad, the eternal pessimist queried.

Who else but Slick could answer that one; which he did with, "Of course they will. And by the time they find out we'll be long gone!"

"Slick, that doesn't make any sense at all," Devon snapped.

"Oh no, here we go again!" I added.

So off we went into the night. Hopefully, we would be in and out of there without doing any damage or, more importantly, getting caught. I don't think I'd be able to turn my story in from the Pender County jail!

*     *     *

"Slick, you DO know that breaking and entering is frowned upon, EVEN in the south; DON'T YOU?"

"Hap you worry too much; and you don't have to whisper. There's no one here to hear you; that is, except for the ghosts," Slick replied.

At that Devon turned to me and in a feigned-trembling voice said, "Are there really ghosts here Hap? You white folk knows how us colored folk is 'bout ghosts an' such things."

"Now cut out that shuck and jive act of yours! And no, there aren't any ghosts here."

To which Slick quickly added, "One."

"Well, one. That is, maybe one. But that's all; and I don't think she does anything but move things around, give you a little shove from behind and other playful things; nothing to be afraid of – I think." I could tell that this did not reassure Devon in the least.

"You think? You mean you don't know? This ghost could be a vengeful, flesh-eating machine and all you can say is, 'you think. Well, if I see her I'm out of here so fast you won't even see the skid marks."

We all had a good laugh at that. We needed a little levity before undertaking what we were about to do.

*      *      *

The house was magnificent in all its old world charm. I would have been very upset if we had as much as moved a doily out of place. So I made it a point to make sure everyone understood that they were to be extra careful not to mess anything up. Since they were doing it for my benefit, I didn't want to have anything happen to this beautiful old house.

There were three floors in this old, beautiful plantation house. There was a half sunken basement, which had windows high up on the walls and a door that had a well with stairs leading up about five or so feet to ground level. This looked to be the servants' quarters and kitchen at one time. There were several rooms that looked like very small bedrooms for the servants and one closet-sized one that appeared to be a washroom for them to clean themselves up in the morning before starting their chores and again at the end of the day.

Just inside of the kitchen area was a flight of stairs that led to the main floor, which sat about five feet above ground level. As you walked down the hall you entered a huge library with built-in shelves, made of beautifully hand-carved wood; they held many volumes of hard-covered books, some dating back into the early 1800s. On this floor there were also several large rooms that were probably used as parlors or studies in the past.

At the top of another staircase, this one made with hand-carved rails and deep, rich wooden stairs, was a large hall that led directly into a large room, probably used for entertaining many guests – such as for a ball. On either side of this room there were three bedrooms with one washroom on either side.

The ceilings in the bedrooms were painted light blue, resembling the sky. The other rooms and hallways had wallpaper made of material with chair-rail trim and crown molding all around.

And there were gas lamps hanging head high on each of the walls; in all, a wonderful old place.

Once we were done staring in wonder at this extraordinary place we took our positions on the three levels and in the out buildings to begin our quest. But first we carefully posted the clues on the wall in the hall as a reminder of what might happen.

As darkness enveloped the old mansion and the grounds surrounding it a misty fog was making its way from Burgaw and blanketing Ravenswood Hall.

*      *      *

Joanna and I were on the first floor with oil lamps in hand, playing our roles, looking for Daddy; when, from outside we could hear a scream. We ran to the library, following the frantic footsteps of the person coming in from one of the out buildings. It was Sunny.

Alfonse and Ada had already seated her in an arm chair and were trying to calm her down. I poured her a glass of Scotch from the decanter that was sitting on the small table next to the fireplace.

"Calm down. Take a deep breath and tell us exactly what you saw," Ada said reassuringly.

"Here, take a drink of this first. It will help calm you," I added. Things were running along smoothly – just as I had written.

"It was Daddy; in the trunk. He's dead!" Sunny said. With that she let out a sigh that left an eerie feeling in my bones. It was as if something had taken over my body and mind. I could see the same in each of the others around me. Something or someone had a hold of us; we were merely players now, dancing to another's tune.

"You stay here with Sunny and Alfonse. We'll go check it out," Delmar said to Ada.

"No. I am going with you. I am his wife."

Ada was not going to be left behind; and neither was Sunny. So off we all went to the garage that held the limo – and

Daddy. But when we arrived there was no blood on the floor or trunk; only Bravo, Daddy's nine-month old Entley puppy licking the ground where Sunny said the blood was before. When we opened the trunk, it was empty.

"Let's all go back and try to figure out the meaning of the rhyme that is on the wall; and try to decipher what the tic-tac- toe message is saying as well," I said.

"Better yet, let's copy it down and each take a piece of it to figure out," Joanna added.

"Yes, let's do that. But Delmar, Mariah and you and I, Joanna, haven't finished our job. Let's leave the riddle-solving to the others while we conduct our searches."

And the four of us went back to our areas while the others sat in the library pouring over the riddles before them. Each in turn, first Delmar in the basement, then Mariah in the bathroom, found Daddy dead. And, each in turn, found that he was no longer there when the others arrived.

Before Joanna and I finished our search we went back to the library to see if the others had come up with any answers to the riddle. We wanted to take another look at these clues to see if we could solve them. They looked like this:

| D | O | A |
|---|---|---|
| A | O | D |
| D | O | A |

> Dad and Ada, Ada and Dad –
> While one life seems taken, the rest will be had. As
> blood flows like syrup; A.O.D. will be he – Before
> day has broken, D.O.A. will he be!

I had it! I knew what it meant. But I dare not tell anyone in case I was wrong. I had to test it out and see if I was right.

"Joanna, I think it's time for us to finish our search in the rooms at the back of the house. Let's go."

"Why are you in such a hurry? We still haven't figured out what that message means."

"Trust me. I think I have an idea as to what it means. Let's go see if I'm right," I said as I grabbed her arm.

As we entered the darkened study at the very back of the first floor we could see something or someone lying on the floor, stretched out. I grabbed an oil lamp sitting on the table near the entrance door and lit the wick. Holding it steadily out in front of us we made our way across the room. Joanna's hand locked onto my arm as we approached.

Suddenly, Joanna gasped and I stopped dead in my tracks. There he was, stretched out on the floor face up with a dagger in his chest; the blood still trickling off of his shirt and onto the floor forming a small pool below his right arm. The handle of the dagger looked strangely like the one that Delmar described that killed, who he thought was, Alfonse when they were at Murrell's Inlet.

I was about to turn and go for the others when I noticed something else that appeared unusual. Joanna must have caught it too because she had started to pull my arm as if to turn me to go out of the room when she stopped and said, "Henry, there's something rotten in the state of Denmark." She loved to quote Shakespeare, especially in a poignant moment like this one.

"I have that same feeling. I want you to go get the others."

"What are you going to do?"

"I'll be fine. I think I know what the clues were saying. Go ahead, get the others. I'll be right here."

"Okay, if you're sure."

"I'm sure. Now go."

*     *     *

"That's it. I've got it. Now let's get out of here before we get caught." I knew how my mystery story had to end.

I sat there while Joanie went back for the others. It was no more than two minutes or so when I saw Brad, Marie and Slick come through the door.

"Where are Susie, Devon and Joanie?" I asked. No one seemed to know.

Just then we heard a loud, blood-curdling scream outside in the long hall that led to the room where we were all congregated. We ran out to see Susie at the top of the stairs holding her hands to her face; still screaming. And there, at the bottom of the landing lay Joanie – lifeless and bleeding.

Marie must have fainted at the sight. Slick reached out and caught her just before she hit the ground. The rest of us stood frozen in our tracks.

From out of one of the bedrooms Devon came running. He looked like he had seen a ghost.

Suddenly, Slick screamed out, "Someone go to her!"

Without thinking I obeyed and ran down the stairs leaping over three or four stairs at a time until I reached the bottom – and Joanie.

"She's still breathing; she's still alive! Thank God," I said as I looked up to the top of the stairs where everyone stood, still holding their breath."

As I said this I saw a strange look steal across Susie's face. I'm not sure what it was, but it looked odd.

But Joanie was unconscious and bleeding. Brad found a phone in the hall and called for an ambulance.

"But we'll be caught for breaking into this place," Susie said without thinking of the situation we were in. I know it struck the others as well as their expressions turned to one of disbelief at what she had just said.

"I'm sorry. I don't know what I was thinking. Of course we need to get help for her immediately," Susie said after seeing the others' reactions.

Susie ran down the stairs as she added, "I've learned a little about first aid since starting the nursing program at school here. Let me help you Hap."

She helped me slow the bleeding and get Joanie into a comfortable position...as she held my hand.

*　　*　　*

It wasn't more than five or so minutes before the emergency vehicle with the paramedics, followed right behind by the Pender County Sheriff, found their way into the plantation house and to where we were all huddled around Joanie.

"Let us take over now," the one paramedic said as he moved me to one side.

After checking her vital signs he said, "She's still with us; but we need to move fast. Please give us room. Who is her husband, partner, whatever?"

"Me," I informed him.

"You can ride with us. I think the Sheriff might have questions for the rest of you. You can meet us at New Hanover Hospital as soon as they release you."

"Hey Slick, ask the deputy that comes to get a hold of Sheriff's Deputy Chuck Walker; you know, the one we call 'Governor'. He's a good guy; he'll help us out of this one.

"Got it, but you just worry about Joanie; I'll handle this."

And off we went. I thought that I might pass out as I sat in the back of the ambulance. One of the paramedics saw that I was flush and about to go down on the floor and broke open a vile of smelling salts and stuck it under my nose. Though it only happens when I see someone I care about injured; that is, ever since my father died.

*     *     *

"Mr. Pozner; I'm Dr. Goodman. I attended your wife when she was admitted and wanted to go over her status with you."

"Thank you, doctor. I'm her, eh, partner; fiancé I guess you'd say. We're not married yet, but we plan to marry soon…" I rambled until he saw my angst and interrupted me.

"Well, what she has is a serious trauma to the brain caused by the fall. We've stopped the bleeding and done several scans and other tests. She's in a coma and we aren't certain for how long, or how serious her injuries are until she comes out of it – IF she comes out of it. I'm sorry to not be able to tell you more, or have better news right now, but…well, if you have a minister or priest that you would like to come I think it would be wise to do that now. We will be monitoring her every minute."

As he stood up to leave he put his hand on my shoulder and concluded with, "She is young and appears to be strong and in good health otherwise; this will work to her benefit. All we can do now is wait…and pray."

# 16

## Living with Reality

**"As Sarge always says, 'Life is like a beer – it's meant to be drunk!'"**
**-Slick**

"Hap, Hap, HAP! Snap out of it. You have to at least let your professor know what's going on so you can get an extension on your story. You've worked too hard and come too far to lose it all now," Slick said as he got in my face.

"I had Susie talk to Joanie's teachers already and they're all letting her skip the exams, since she's a straight 'A' student. She'll have time to recuperate before she starts her senior year in the fall.

But I lost all interest in my story, my graduation, myself. Most of the last 24 hours I spent at her bedside...waiting. Slick had talked me into going home for a change of clothes and something to eat. But, as for school and work; I no longer cared.

I had lost my dad just when we were beginning to know each other. I couldn't take it if I lost Joanie just when we were finding a future together.

"Look Hap, she's going to pull through this. Everything's gonna be okay. I know it," Slick said reassuringly.

"When she comes back to us and all you've done is sit here and mope what do you think the first words out of her mouth will be? Yeh, that's right. She's gonna say, 'And what have you been doing while I was busy in a coma fixing my broken parts – huh? Sure, you've been sitting around with that no good slouch, Slick, waiting for me to tell you to get off of your asses and get busy with life!'"

As depressed as I was, that remark caused me to began to laugh at his absurdity. Then I began to cry.

"What will I do, Slick."

"No Hap. What will WE do. We're in this together. Susie and I love her like you do. We've been through life together so far; and we can't let it end here. As Sarge always says, 'Life is like a beer – it's meant to be drunk!'"

When he said this I think I finally got it. Maybe I've been around him and his family too long; or maybe there is some wisdom to their sayings. But I finally get it – and he's right.

"Now I'll let the people at your job know that you'll be out for a while, but you should call that professor yourself. I'm sure he can give you an extension, or make some arrangements to help out."

"Thanks Slick. I guess you're right."

At this he interjected, "It's about time you admitted it."

"Now don't go getting a big head; excuse me, a bigger head!"

We both burst out in laughter. I don't know if it was the humor or just the tension exploding; but we both needed it.

"But I want you to know that I'm only doing this because I don't want to have to face Joanie when she come to. Got it."

"Of course, Hap. I understand," he said with a grin.

*    *    *

I got my extension, the folks at work gave me an indefinite leave, and Slick and I spent most of our time at the hospital watching over Joanie. Susie would appear at least twice a week during her free time, but didn't seem to be as concerned as we were. Maybe it was because she was in a nursing program and knew something we didn't. She did, however, visit Joanie more often when she worked in the hospital as part of the practical experience for the classes she took.

# 17

## Writer's Block

**"And we'll still be your friend when you're nobody – SPECIAL"**
**-Slick**

Sitting here just watching her for hours on end is worse than almost anything. It reminds me of sitting in the hospital room with my father, watching him and hoping for the best. I know I shouldn't think about it, because this is different; Joanie WILL be well again. I guess it's times like these that bring out the best, or the worst, in people. It's also the time when I seem to get ideas for writing. As I stare at her as she seems so peaceful, quietly sleeping my thought drift of and words begin to flow through my pen; words that reflect the moment and how I see the two of us, and what I hope for our future.

\*       \*       \*

## Thoughts of You

Scattered thoughts, random memories —
That's all that I can see.
Sunken hopes, dreams detached —
Feeling blue; sad for you and me.

Childhood days give way to things —
That crowds our narrow view.
When times like these release my mind —
I'm left with thoughts of you.

\*     \*     \*

"Slick, what are you doing here now? Aren't you supposed to be in class, or at work?"

"Hap, today is Saturday. Get with it man. Saturday is my day of rest." He just laughed as he said this.

"I thought that Sunday is the day of rest?"

"Yeh, but I need two days, so I start on Saturday; ha." "How's she doing; any signs of her coming around yet?" Slick got serious for a moment. I think he cares about Joanie as much as I do; only he looks at her as more of the sister he never had.

"No, but the doctors said not to expect anything for at least a few days, if not weeks," I responded holding my head in my hands from lack of sleep.

"Hap, you have got to get away from here, for a little while at least. You sit here, sleep here; I'd even say eat here – if you were eating at all. Now I'm here everyday; and Susie's here at least three or four times a week between her visits and when she's here for her classes. We won't leave her alone. Now go home, get some food and sleep a while; and for God's sake take a shower. I'll stay here 'till you get back. And don't come back until you look and smell human again; got it?" Slick said with a smile.

"Alright already! I'll go; but so you don't think that I just sit here and stare I want you to read some of what I've been writing while I'm waiting for Joanie to come around…and, no, It's not the ending to my story. It's some poems that I'm writing for her – and some for you guys as well. It's going to be my first collection of poems that I hope to publish as soon as I graduate."

I could see Slick starting to smile as I said this. He has always been my best cheerleader when it comes to my hopes for a writing career.

"And when I become famous from my writing I'll remember all of the little people who were my friend when I was nobody!" I said trying to inject a bit of the Graham [Slick's] family's wit into the conversation.

Not to be outdone Slick responded with, "And we'll still be your friend when you're nobody – SPECIAL!"

"Okay. Why do I even try? Here's a poem I wrote last night. I guess the light from the full moon shining down on her reminded me of that night at Zoar Valley; you remember just after high school graduation. It was when you all went to bed and Joanie and I sat together in front of the dying campfire.

\*    \*    \*

## Sometimes

Sometimes when I hold you; there are no words to say –
Sometimes when I touch you; the night becomes the day.
Sometimes when I see you; the light shines just on you –
It's only when I'm with you; my life begins anew.

Sometimes the moon sits; along your gentle smile –
Sometimes your still voice; asks the question 'why?'
Sometimes your thoughts break; the time we had now gone –
They're vague and distant memories; shadows in the sky.

\*    \*    \*

After reading several more I could see, as he listened to them that Slick was having some deep thoughts of his own…imagine that.

"Okay. What's wrong? I can see you're not too happy with my poems."

"Well Hap; to be honest I'm not. They're good, don't get me wrong. I do like them; but they're all somber. Can't you liven it up a bit? Joanie's gonna say the same thing when she reads them. Unless, of course, your writing 'a book of poems to cry about'. Please tell me you're not."

"I guess you have a point there. I imagine the lack of sleep and food combined with seeing her just lying there kinda put me in that kind of mood."

"Not to mention the lack of a good shower!" Slick threw in.

"Anyway; I suppose Joanie would like me to write some more upbeat ones as well – especially when I know she's going to be okay. Right?"

I could see Slick begin to smile as he slapped me on the back and said, "That's the spirit. Now go home and do what I told you. Come back – but not before six tonight. I'll be here waiting. Then you can get a start on writing some of your happier poems; and they'll be done just in time for Joanie to wake up and read them. So get a move on!"

Sometimes you can't argue with logic…even Slick's kind of logic.

\*       \*       \*

As the days began to blend into one another and become nothing more than a blur, I found solitude in the fact that she was still with me. I also found comfort in knowing that I had good friends who were there when I need them; and sometimes when I didn't.

I think it was Thursday, about a week and a half after the accident that Susie and Slick came to the hospital to visit. It was early morning; about eight o'clock, which surprised me. I didn't know Slick to ever get up that early – even in high school. I suppose that was one of the reasons it took him five years to graduate!

"Well, good morning to you both. Slick you look half asleep," I said as they came into the room.

"Yeh, well you know who made me do it; and I don't mean the devil!"

"He sleeps too much. Between that and watching cartoons and listening to his ONE Grateful Dead album I'm surprised he has time to go to class or work."

"I'm a man of many talents. I can do all of that and still take care of school and work. Why I think the National Geographic is looking to do a special on me. You remember how they inducted me as a member when we were kids, don't ya?"

Susie and I just looked at each other; she rolled her eyes and sighed.

"Ah, Slick I hate to burst your bubble; but they sent that letter to every kid in the country. I got one, Susie got one, Joanie got one - why, the whole damn world got one. We just hated to tell you then – you were so proud to be asked to join, we couldn't bring ourselves to tell you."

He paused for a moment to catch his breath at this news. Then he smiled, shook his head and began laughing and said, "I get it; you guys are making this up because you're jealous. That's okay. I can take a joke."

Susie and I looked at each other and then at Slick. We knew it was useless.

"Ya got us. Hap was just trying to mess with you," Susie said, knowing it was hopeless.

"Well how is she? We didn't come here to talk about me; now did we?" Slick said.

"She hasn't stirred. But I know she's getting better. The doctors say that her brain activity has begun to increase, and she's showing signs of improvement."

Instead of talking more about Joanie or sitting by her side Susie said something that struck me as very odd.

"Hap; I heard you've been writing some more poems while you've been here. Can I hear some of them? I just love how you write. I hope you wrote one for me this time. Did you?"

"Well, as a matter of fact, I have been writing some; and I did write one for you. Would you like to hear a few of them?"

"We'd love to; wouldn't we Slick?"

I could see Susie poke Slick, who was now staring at Joanie and rubbing her hand. He jumped a bit and looked back at us.

"Sure. Let's hear them."

"Okay. This first one I wrote is kind of about life and what we sometimes miss – today."

\*     \*     \*

## This Day of Our Life

Some say life happens when we're young;
While others when we're old.
It's all too much; it's such a fix –
Yet this is what I'm told.

But simplify to one hard fact;
It's something dogs all know.
Life happens to us every day –
Need all we do is show.

We grieve about our 'have dones';
And fret about 'our wills'.
When all we have is 'doing'
To help us climb our hills.

Yesterdays are practices for what we do today;
Tomorrows never get here – they never see their way.
Today is what we have for now; the curse of all our strife;
The joy of which becomes for us –
                In sum; this day of our life.

\*       \*       \*

"Better than the last one you read to me; but no cigar –
as they say."

My biggest critic, Slick. Who would have imagined.

"Okay; then how about this. I can't imagine you can find fault with this – it's about you!"

"Well it's about time you recognized my talent; my charisma, my 'jeux de vie' as it were."

"You amaze me sometimes. You barely got through two years of German, which took you three years, with my help I might add; and now you're speaking French? Give me a break!" "I'll have you know you're not the only one who has helped with my education. As you may or may not recall, Susie took four years of French in high school..."

At this Susie interrupted with, "Yeh; and I did it in four years!"

Slick just looked at her and continued, "Since we've been living here she's been tutoring me in French."

"Okay; I'll bite. Why is she doing it – and more importantly, why do you want to learn to speak French? The French hate us you know."

Susie chimed in, "We're planning on going to Paris as soon as we can scrap up the cash. Just for a few months or so. Maybe get a Eurail pass and see some other counties as well. You know kinda bum around Europe for a while."

I had to add, "Should I send them all a warning letter that you're coming?"

"Well?" Slick said with a look of 'let's move on'.

"Well what?" He had me so confused I didn't know what in the hell was going on now.

~ 113 ~

"Are you going to read the poem about me or aren't you?"

"Alright, here goes."

\*       \*       \*

## Moccasins are Shoes Too

Shoe:
Somehow they don't look quite the same;
They haven't been heeled or soled.
They're hard to get on, and harder to get off;
And they smell from new to old.

If you wear them long they wear right out;
If you don't they dry out and crack.
Unless they're on they have no shape;
What are they good for? They're crap!

Moccasin:
It's many moons we've been around;
And served our purpose well.
It's many men that wore with pride;
Our value I will tell.

On many a hunt in silent stealth;
My people have us worn.

With many a mile on foot we've walked;
And many a load we've borne.

Wisdom:
It's true I know, these things you say;
They don't sing, shine or last.
My people wear them not for this;
Their time is not yet passed.

A caution brother it's not to judge;
What for my world is true.
For all the years and all we do;
Moccasins are shoes too!

\*　　　\*　　　\*

A puzzled look hung on his face; I couldn't tell whether he loved it or hated it; Susie just starting laughing hysterically.

After what seemed like a long silence, he said, "Okay; I don't get it. You said it was about me. So where is the part about me?" Slick said in an agitated tone.

I could see that Slick was not only confused, but a bit annoyed by my poem; so I figured it would be better if I explained.

"It's an analogy. You know – I'm comparing you to a pair of old moccasins."

"Oh, that's much better. Of course, I get it now. And this is supposed to what…make me feel good?"

"No. You're missing the point."

"I guess I am, oh great poet. What exactly am I missing? That I'm like an old, smelly pair of moccasins? No wait; my whole family is like an old, smelly pair – right?"

All the while Susie kept laughing; so much so that tears began to run down her cheeks. This only made Slick more agitated.

"Stop already! That's not what I meant by this. Look it; You, and your family if you like, are not like everyone else; but you are unique and important in ways that are…well, important." "Keep going; you're digging. I'm not sure if it's deeper or your way out. Even Sarge would like hearing this explanation." "What I mean by this is that you may not seem like everyone else; and maybe, to some, you don't seem to fit – you are vital to me as my friend. You have always been that one person – or thing in this case – that has been there to help."

"Okay; enough. You got yourself out of that one. But do me a favor, would ya?" Slick said.

"Sure; anything," I responded with a smile. "Don't tell anyone that you wrote that for me."

With that he busted out in laughter; and I followed him. After a few minutes I said, "I've got a few more. Do you want to hear the one I wrote for you, Susie?"

Her laughter stopped abruptly and she smartly responded, "Not if you value your life!"

"Oh, come on. It's not like that last one. Slick, how about you? Do you want to hear any more of the poems I wrote?"

Slick just looked at me and said, "Not if they're about me!"

*      *      *

It was two weeks before we saw any signs that she was coming out of her coma. At first it was only slight twitching of the fingers and toes; then movement of her lips and eyelids. Then the breakthrough came – she opened her eyes for the first time since her fall.

# 18

## The Awakening

**"Tomorrow brings new hope to life; today brings all the joy."**
**-Hap**

"Tada!" Joanie said in a somewhat groggy state.

"Tada!" I said right back to her as she said her first word in two weeks.

"I guess you haven't forgotten the old line we always said whenever we got hurt playing circus as kids, did you?" She smiled as she reminded me.

"How could I? We were 'The Flying Wallendas of the Ringling Brothers Circus, weren't we," I shot back with a smile and a tear in my eye to see her smile at me once again.

"Don't ever do that stunt again; promise me. We thought we had lost you. And we couldn't, that is I couldn't, go on without you."

She just grinned and responded, "And what would you do? Kill yourself? Well, I wouldn't let you; even if I were dead. Got it mister?"

I smiled back as she added, "Oh, and by the way; did you finish your story, or do I have to do that for you too?"

"Slick said you'd say that," I mumbled under my breath.

"What was that? Don't mumble at me," she said giving me a stern glair.

"Nothing," I responded happy she didn't hear me. "As a matter of fact I did finish it. But I have to admit I wouldn't have without Slick's intervention."

"Now that's a good one. Tell me more." She couldn't believe my words; so I told her about the little talk he had with me.

"I guess I owe him one – but he still can't move back in with us...ever!" she said trying now to sit up. I could see that her head hurt as she tried to do this so I made her stay lying down.

"You stay lying down; you're not in any condition to be sitting up and moving around yet. Besides, I wanted to catch you at a weak moment so that I could read a couple of poems I wrote to go into my first collection of poetry to be published someday. I figured if I read them to you while you were in a coma it would be like reading to Slick, so I thought I'd wait until you came around. And here you are...and here they are (showing her my poems). What do ya say?"

"I guess I'm your captive audience. But if they stink I'm pressing the buzzer and getting you ejected from my room. No pressure though."

"No pressure? Well, here goes…This first one I wrote for Susie. Oddly enough she didn't want to hear it."

\*      \*      \*

### Stormy Seas

I see you like the ocean, with beauty vast and deep;
Beneath your rocky cover lie, mysteries that you keep.
As depth and darkness follow one, unto the ocean floor;
The multitude of life you bring, are wanting yet for more.

The winds that blow, the tides that surge, are just reminders of;
The ebb and flow throughout your life, the promise of your love.
Yet from these torrents raging, within your bowels deep;
A beauty lies within your heart, it's there still fast asleep.

\*      \*      \*

I waited for a reaction, but got none.

"Okay; so what do you think? You're not saying anything. Come on."

"I'm thinking. Read another one; then I tell you what I think. That's what I think!" Joanie said as she attempted to cross her arms in protest to my cajoling.

"It's a good thing you're incapacitated or I'd have to give you a good thrashing lady," I said playfully; just happy to see her with me again.

"How about this one; it's a poem I wrote for you. It's kind of a metaphor for some of the quirky things I love about you"

"Quirky. Huh? You have no reason to talk mister!"

"Slow down. Don't get into a thither. You know a good hospital thither costs five times more than the ones you can get on the street nowadays."

That calmed her down. She just rolled her eyes and said, "Okay, let's hear it. But it better be at least as good as the one you wrote for Susie or you'll be the next one in the hospital."

"So does that mean you liked it? I could make it a little longer if you think that it needs it. Then again maybe I should shorten it a bit. What do you think?"

She just smiled coyly and said, "Just read!" She wasn't about to satisfy my curiosity. "Alright, so I guess you'll tell me later; right?"

At that she added, "I'm already in pain. Would you please just read the damn thing!"

I knew by that last remark that I had pushed a little too hard, too soon; so I moved on to the poem with, "This is called, "Without You"".

*     *     *

## Without You

The world would never miss your every task;
Or beg the question that no one else dare ask.
It never sees the change of mood from left to right;
Your strong will leaves it little chance for flight.

The world upon your shoulders you must bear;
The rest of us don't seem too much to care.
Without you hope would never rise above;
But with you what we cherish is your love.

\*     \*     \*

Before I had a chance to get her critique I saw her looking over my shoulder in the direction of the door. She must have been there for a few minutes because, as I turned around I could see that the nurse was standing just inside the room.

As I smiled at her she said, "Well I liked it. That was a lovely poem he wrote for you." She had come in when she saw by the monitors at her station that there was some activity. I guess since Joanie and I were talking she didn't interrupt; but now she did.

"You'll have to leave for a few moments. The doctor is on his way and will need to examine her. I'll call you back when we're finished." She turned toward Joanie, dismissing me, "Well, it's so nice to see you back with us. I trust you've had enough rest," she said with a faint laugh.

"I think everything is going to be alright," Joanie said as I turned to leave the ICU.

"I think you're right," was all that I could muster between tears of joy. I guess being overtired, in addition to her surprise awakening and appearance, had caught up with me. It was probably best that I was leaving the room; that will give me time to get myself together.

Slick was still sitting in the waiting room working on a crossword puzzle where I left him hours ago.

"Hap. What's a four letter word for lucky?"

"Tada!" was the only word I uttered, knowing that it would tell it all.

Slick nodded, wrote it in the box, and then looked up with a big smile on his face. He understood my message, jumped out of his chair and hugged me laughing and jabbering away.

I said, "Slow down, slow down. Let's go get some coffee; I'll explain it all at the café."

# 19

## A Deadline Missed

**"Why buy the eggs when you can steal the chicken."**
-Slick

"Hap, Hap, HAP! Do you have any idea what time it is!"

"Joanie, I don't even know what day it is," was my sorry reply. I had fallen asleep in the chair next to her bed as I did many nights that she has been in the hospital.

"And by the way, how is your head?"

"It hurts a little, but I'll live...I guess. Now you'd better get up and get your story in to Prof. Hartley 'cause you only have one hour to get it in or it will be late. I think he might not be as kind as to give you an extension on your extension."

"Thanks for getting me up; I can still make the deadline. If I don't get this in on time my life will be ruined. I will go down in history as infamous. My children will be cursed for generations to come..."

"Enough of the drama; 'get 'er dun' my little southern man or I'll never marry you and you will end up with Bobby Jo Trailer-trash, her seven illegitimate kids and living with your in- laws in a singlewide in the Great Dismal Swamp. Get it."

"Yeh, I get your point. It's a good thing you're laid up in that hospital bed or I'd…Wait a minute…did you say you'll never marry me? Was that a proposal? If it was, you know I'll have to think about it first."

"If you want to live long enough to graduate you'd better shut your pie-hole right now…And maybe it was a proposal," she quipped with a smirk on her face.

"Mmm…"

# 20

## Trial by Fire

"Once you finish the job, it's over!"
-Slick

"Hap, Hap, HAP! Are you listening to me?"

"Yes, of course Professor Hartley. I'm hanging on your every word."

"Good. As I've said over and over, 'I haven't wasted a one.' Do you understand young man?"

"Now you know what a stickler I am with deadlines. But I'll be honest with you since this is your last course of your last year here. And, quite frankly, I'll have you disemboweled if you tell anyone a word of what I'm about to tell you…"

"I'm sorry; you'll have 'my what' cut off?"

"Anyway, what I mean to say is I do this simply to scare students. You know, they won't know what you've said if you don't have their attention; sort of the Machiavellian philosophy.

But I will tell you in all candor, you have been one of my very best writers in all of my years of teaching. If you ever need a reference or recommendation please be sure to use my name. By the way, I certainly hope your girlfriend is doing well."

"Thank you. She's doing much better now." I guess he's not all 'Heartless'.

"Now, would you be so kind as to read the synopsis of your story, followed by the first and last chapters. I will read the rest at my leisure. Grade corrections are due tomorrow – you see I also have deadlines; and I wanted to give you as much time as possible to finish this project given your unusual circumstances."

With an air of self-satisfaction he continued, "It would be impossible for me to read each student's story in its entirety before my deadline so your grade will be based upon what I hear today. But don't worry, I will read those I haven't finished over the summer. And I do have one final opportunity to change a grade before the next semester begins. However, I've been doing it this way for many years and have found that I have been correct in my grading 99.9% of the time."

I took a deep breath as I began, "Alright. Here goes…"

After I had finished I took a deep breath and waited to hear what he had to say. He actually was pretty nice about it. He even took the time to go over some areas that he thought needed revision.

"Hap; I'm taking the time to go through this with you because I believe that this is something, given a bit more work, would be very marketable. In fact, we have a university press right here on our campus. I'd be glad to help it along if you're interested. But first you'll need to take it home and go over it with a fine-toothed comb before you even think of submitting it for publication. What do you think about that?"

I was floored.

"Absolutely; I'd love to have it published here at UNC-W!"

We went over the process and I left flying high all the way home.

# 21

## And in the End...

**"Nah; it's water up a duck's ass!"**
-Slick

"Is someone having a party and I wasn't invited?"

"Very funny, Hap. You know why all of our friends are here; they're waiting to hear the ending to your story. And, by the way, did you get your grade for it; or do we have to wait on that as well?"

I could see, in Joanie's crowded hospital room, all of our friends who were accomplices in our little adventure; gathered to hear the end to my murder mystery.

"I've got good news on both counts. I got my grade and I think you will all like the ending. I'm going to save the grade until after I read the final chapters. Ready?" In

unison they all shouted, "Yeh!"

"Well, here goes...I think this is about where we left off at our Ravenswood adventure a few weeks ago..."

\*     \*     \*

"But where's Henry?" Robert asked.

"He stayed in the room. He said he has the answer to the riddle. You all go; I'll stay here with Alfonse and Sunny. We'll be right behind you," responded Joanna.

We all raced through the long hall of the first floor and into the back study where Henry and Joanna had found Daddy…that is, all except for Sunny, Joanna and Alfonse. Alfonse was having one of his 'episodes' and needed to sit a moment and drink some water. All the excitement must have gotten to him. But there we were…and there they were – Daddy and Henry. Daddy was sitting on a chair, laughing and drinking a glass of wine with Henry; blood still on his shirt and on the floor next to where he sat.

I gasped at the sight and exclaimed, "What is going on here? Are you alright? What happened?"

With that Daddy put down his glass and calmly stated, "Would all of you please sit down and let me explain. That is, let us explain; right Henry?"

"Sure Daddy. You see when I saw Bravo licking the floor near the limo earlier I found that odd. I could see that all of you noticed it too; but, I think, you erred in discounting that. He wouldn't be trying so hard to get a taste of whatever was on that floor unless it was something that he found tasty. In this case it was something that was made to look like blood. So after you left

I took a closer look at the spot that he was licking and saw some residue of what appeared to be red on the concrete floor. I was able to scrape up just enough with my pocket knife to get a taste of what it was. It tasted like syrup."

Henry proceeded to explain the riddle next.

"Now going back to the library and taking a closer look at the rhyme that was on the wall I tried to put it in another context. What if this is a riddle for us to unravel; **a spoof** of some sort?"

I could see everyone's eyes begin to light up as he spelled it out. It was our 'ah-ha moment'.

"Take the first couplet of the rhyme: 'Dad and Ada, Ada and Dad – While one life seems taken, the rest will be had.' Don't you get it? It doesn't say 'While one life IS taken' or 'the OTHER will be had'; it says 'SEEMS taken' and 'the REST'. One life will only SEEM taken – not really taken; and the REST - that's us; you and me, not just Ada or Daddy."

Henry could see that we weren't all following his thought process; so he stopped and began a different tact.

"Okay. If it only SEEMS that Daddy, for instance, is dead, and we buy it, then we've been had!"

It all made sense to us now.

"But what about the next two lines and the pictograph?" Mariah spoke up.

"Let me go back to the tic-tac-toe graph. It does spell out Dad and Ada, as well as D.O.A., or Dead On Arrival. However D.O.A. can also stand for Dead Or Alive! – like on the old, Wild West wanted posters. This is to say, he might be DEAD, or he

~ 131 ~

might just as easily be ALIVE. And it also spells out A.O.D. across the middle. Now, we know what the first part means – Daddy and Ada might be killed if we didn't figure out the clues in time; but the last part stumped me. That is, until I had a chance to talk with Daddy a few moments ago. But I'll let him tell that part and more, after I finish the riddle for you."

We were all spellbound by his astute analysis. I could see that Daddy was impressed as well.

"The last two lines state, 'As blood flows like syrup, A.O.D. will be he – Before day has broken, D.O.A. will he be!'. That's when I put two and two together. Bravo was licking some kind of syrup. The riddle was telling us that. I have to admit the
'A.O.D. will be he' and the 'D.O.A. will he be' had me stumped. Then I remembered how, first Sunny found Daddy in the trunk of the limo, and not 10 or so minutes after we checked it out Delmar found him hanging from a rafter in the basement. Then, when Ada and some of the others went to see if Mariah was okay she told them that he was floating facedown in the bath tub. Then, of course, Joanna and I found him here."

I could see by the other's expressions that he had piqued our curiosity with this.

"I knew, at this point that there had to be someone else in on this. Daddy could not have been in all of those places as quickly as he seemed to be. Then it occurred to me; what if every other appearance was someone else, someone he trusts and someone whose absence would go unnoticed by the rest of us. And someone roughly the same height, build, age, and someone who knew this place like the back of his hand. There are secret passages and hidden hallways in this place. Then it hit me – Davenport!"

At this point Daddy put his hand on Henry's arm as if to say 'I'll take it from here'.

"Yes, Henry is exactly right – **'THE BUTLER DID IT!'**. Ha, ha!"

After that you could see the tension break and everyone began to laugh along with Daddy.

"You see the D.O.A. means more than Dead On Arrival. It is also my initials as they would be written somewhat military style – (Daddy) Orwatt, Arthur. What Henry couldn't figure out, even though he did determine that Davenport was my accomplice, is what the A.O.D. stood for. Those are his initials – (Albert) Osborn, Davenport. You see how they were both what you call…oh Ada, what's that expression."

"Do you mean 'double entendre' dear?"

"Why yes of course, that's it. Those initials were 'double entendre's'. I can't fault Henry for not knowing that."

Mariah spoke up at this point, "But what was the purpose of putting us all through this ordeal – even your wife Ada?"

"Yes. I must apologize for keeping you in the dark dear Ada. But I couldn't reveal this part of my plan even to you. THIS was the final test to determine who my new president would be. I needed someone with an analytical mind; someone who was not afraid to get their hands dirty, so to speak. It was imperative for me to select the right person; and I did – it is, of course Henry.

~ 133 ~

He was the only one who, not only figured out the ruse, but he also went out on a limb by himself by protecting the rest of you from any fallout if he was wrong. I need a person who will have that kind of courage running my businesses; someone, like 'Give- em-hell Harry, who told us, 'the buck stops here'. As to the rest of you, don't feel badly. You are here because you all possess a great many skills that I, and now Henry, need in order for this operation to thrive. You are all important members of my team."

"I think I understand this part of the night's events, but what about the weird happenings during our trips in and around the Wilmington area?" Delmar puzzled.

"As I mentioned when this all began I really did intend for that part of it to help Ada get ideas for her book. But, as to the strange occurrences that you all got caught up in I don't have an answer to that."

I felt it was time for me to clear thing up at this point, "I think I can answer that for all of you."

I could see everyone turn first their eyes, and then their bodies in my direction as if to give me their undivided attention and to gain some insight into their confusion.

"I will admit I did know about this whole thing weeks ago; in enough time to make my plans. Sorry Daddy; my inquisitive nature and 'mystery writing' instincts led me to snoop around when I saw a memo you left laying around indicating that you were planning a little adventure here. As you know Wilmington is a place filled with ghost stories; some based on historic events, some on legend and sightings. So I used these ghost stories and legends and hired actors from DeLaurentis Studio, here in town, to set the wheels in motion."

"But it all seemed so real. How did you manage to pull that off?" Brent asked.

"You'd be surprised what special effects people can do!" I replied

Robert spoke up, "Wait a minute. I still have a whole bunch of questions that haven't been answered yet."

"All in good time, all in good time. But right now I'd like to get into a dry shirt. Why don't I meet you all in the breakfast room where Davenport and Clarissa can serve us the wonderful breakfast that Mrs. Higgins has prepared for us. Oh, and don't worry; there isn't anything in it that might harm you. Is there Davenport?"

"I certainly hope not sir…"

# 22

## But I'm Innocent Your Honor!

**"My family is famous for our Idiot-matic expressions!"**
**-Slick**

"Wait; what about Alfonse, Joanna and Sunny?" Brent asked.

We had all gotten so wrapped up in this mystery that we forgot that three of our party were still missing. It was just then that we heard it.

**"Ahhh!"**

We heard a scream, and then the sound of someone running toward us in a panic. It was Sunny. From the expression on her face we thought that she had seen a ghost.

"Come quickly. Hurry now! It's Joanna; there at the bottom of the stairs."

We followed her with candles in hand. There at the bottom of the stairs, as Sunny had said lay Joanna – limp and lifeless.

"Quick. Get down there to her. See if she is still alive!" I screeched.

Henry was the first to get to her. He gently and slowly picked up her head. We could see the blood pouring out of the side of it. Even in the dim light I could see the death stare in her eyes; a look of absence and yet of panic.

Henry lowered his head and began to weep over, what was now, the shell of a once beautiful and spirited woman. She was dead.

Mariah, who was the last to enter the hall and see Joanna lying at the bottom of the stairs in Henry's arms, swooned and began to fall to the hardwood floor below her feet. Just as she was about to hit it Delmar reached over and caught her.

Daddy was quick to call Davenport over and have him call an ambulance in the hopes that there was still an ounce of life in her.

"Sunny. What happened?" Mariah spoke up after she came to and regained her composure.

"I don't know. I was in the library with Alfonse and Joanna. Then Alfonse asked me for directions back to the room where you all just went to. I told him and he left. Joanna said that she needed to get back and I told her that I would be along in a moment or two. I needed to sit for a minute after the trying ordeal of this evening. It was then that I heard a thud and what sounded like something, or someone, rolling down the stairs. I got up and ran out to see a shadow racing down the hall toward one of the bedrooms; that one over there," Sunny said as she pointed to the room opposite the one where we were all gathered a few moments ago.

She continued, "I ran out to see what it was. Holding my candle up I could see the bust of Diogenes on the floor at the top of the stairs and a figure curled up at the bottom. That's when I realized that it was Joanna. Of course, I screamed as I dropped my candle."

At this Brent walked over and picked up the bust that was lying there and then quickly dropped it.

"There's blood all over it!" he shrieked.

Meanwhile Delmar went over to the bedroom that Sunny was still pointing to. He peered inside with his candle in front of him, bent down, seemed to pick something up out of a waste basket just inside the door.

"Ah ha!" he exclaimed.

Delmar approached us with what appeared to be a bloody handkerchief with the initials A. D.O. embroidered on it.

"I think I know who this belongs to," he said with a look of anger on his face.

"I know who it belongs to because I bought it for him...Alfonse DeMario Odell!"

Just as Delmar spit these words out, from out of the shadows Alfonse appeared.

"What's going on? Why is everyone standing around here? I get so lost in big houses like this. Oh my God – what happened to Joanna. Is she alright...I think I'm going to faint."

With that he fell to the floor in a swoon.

"As soon as he comes to I'm going to kill him. I'm waiting so he can witness it!"

Delmar rushed toward Alfonse, but Henry and Brent grabbed him and stopped him before he could get to Alfonse.

Mariah bent over and lifted Alfonse's head as he was coming to.

"How did that happen? What's going on?" Alfonse asked.

"I'll tell you what happened..." Delmar began as he lifted himself from the floor where the two had tackled him.

"You hit Joanna over the head and pushed her down the stairs; then you used this handkerchief to wipe the blood from your hands. You panicked and ran to the nearest room and put it in the trash basket thinking no one would find it. And finally, you hid in the shadows as Sunny came from the library on her way to meet up with us. After you heard us all coming this way, you came out and feigned surprise at what we had discovered." Delmar paused. You could see his body change from one full of rage to one full of sadness.

"But why; did you think you were helping me? Did you find out that Joanna had warned me about you? Was it revenge, love; why Alfonse?" Delmar broke down in tears.

"I didn't do it! I would never harm her. And yes I knew that she had talked to you about me. She came to me and told me that she did. But I didn't hold a grudge. I know she was just looking out for you...as a friend. I understood her concerns. I didn't kill her; I swear!" Alfonse turned toward the bottom of the stairs and just stared at Joanna's lifeless body in Henry's arms.

# 23

## The Investigation

"In a perfect world – I'd leave."
-Slick

The ambulance had arrived with the paramedics. They were trying to get Joanna's body out of Henry's arms. She was taken to the hospital and pronounced D.O.A., dead on arrival. So they waited for the police to arrive.

At this Daddy spoke up, "I believe it important that we touch nothing and we don't discuss anything until the police get here. I've had Davenport call them and they will be here momentarily."

Within a few minutes the doorbell rang and it was the police; two detectives to be exact: one middle-aged man, around fiftyish, and one young woman – probably in her early thirties. They were detectives Iverson and MacCallum respectively.

You could almost laugh, if there were anything to laugh about. He took out a small notepad and pencil stub, while she pulled out a micro recorder for her notes – telling signs of their ages.

They were followed by a team of crime scene investigators who got busy right away going over the area for evidence.

"While Detective MacCallum goes over the site with the forensic team, I'm going to have to ask all of you to please have a seat in the library and not talk to each other so that I can get information from each of you one at a time. Mr. Orwatt; is there a room that I could use for my interrogation?" Detective Iverson said in a commanding voice.

"Of course; you may use any room you like. There are eight other rooms on this floor and more on the second and lower levels as well." Always the cordial host; even in a crisis.

"I will be asking each of you questions about what occurred here today. At this point you are witnesses. If you feel that you will need a lawyer for any reason you should call one now. I won't read anyone their rights since you are not suspects – yet," Iverson added.

"If, at some point, you DO become a suspect I will let you know, and then I will read you your Miranda Rights. This may have been an accident; it may have been a homicide. That's what we're here to find out."

"Detective, I can save you the trouble of this investigation. I know who killed Joanna. It was…" Delmar began to speak, but was interrupted.

"Delmar; I think that the good detective can do his job without our trying to micro-manage HIS investigation," Henry blurted out.

"Now if you don't mind being the first one, Mr. Delmar; would you follow me and we'll have a nice chat about what you know and what you only think you know." Iverson was not going to let a civilian take over his investigation; as well intended as he might be.

"Delmar's my first name; Pickett is my last name; but you may call me Delmar, detective."

"Thank you, Delmar. Now, if you will come with me. This shouldn't take very long," Iverson said as he took Delmar's arm and directed him to the next room.

He interviewed each of us in turn leaving Alfonse and Sunny until the end. They were the only ones out of the room when Joanna fell down the stairs.

After he and the rest of the team were finished Iverson addressed us all as we sat in shock in the library, "I'd like all of you to stay around Wilmington for a few days; at least until our investigation is complete. I have all of your information – names, addresses, etc. – so I'll be in touch. And please don't discuss this with anyone; not each other, your friends, family, neighbors – and especially the press. We'll handle them. Thank you for your cooperation."

At this Iverson came over to Daddy and me and asked, "Would it be possible for the three of us get together tomorrow after all of the reports are in, say around noon for a private conversation about some things that I'm not too clear on?" He turned to leave, paused for a moment, and then turned back to us and added, "Oh, and I'll have my partner Detective MacCallum there as well."

"Why, of course detective. Anything to help find out what happened to our beloved friend Joanna," I responded.

The next 24 hours seemed like an eternity. Daddy insisted that everyone stay the night. He called his personal physician and had him come to the house with his nurse to make sure everyone was okay. He had him give them something so that they could rest; especially Henry who was still in a state of shock.

Davenport, meanwhile, had driven over to the morgue and then to the funeral parlor to make the necessary arrangements.

The doctor gave Henry a sedative which seemed to help him relax enough to go to his room and lie down for a while.

After a few hours rest Henry came out of his room and into the dining room where everyone else had gathered and announced, "I know it might seem rash or reactive on my part, but I have decided that I cannot take the position as president of Orwatt Enterprises. Yes, it has a lot to do with Joanna's death; but it has as much to do with my realization that I need to change the direction of my life as well."

With that he turned and walked out of the room, went back to his bedroom and locked the door.

We all sat there stunned for quite a long time. Finally, Daddy broke the silence with, "I think I understand what Henry just did. I have to admire him for his vision in such troubling times. All the more reason he was the right pick for the position; but I will honor his decision."

"But what will you do about the position?" Mariah interjected.

"I could just continue on as it has been and wait a while to think it over. But that would mean I would be untrue to myself. And it would cause all of you more anguish and worry over who will take the helm. I always have a plan B; and this time is   no exception. I have to say that my plan B in no way diminishes this person's, or any of the rest of your, ability to lead my companies. I want you to keep in mind that I am entrusting a great deal of my life's work into the hands of someone in this room; and I would never do that if that person was an 'also ran'. I know that my choice is a good one."

"I think that this is all happening too fast for me," I said.

"Sunny. Would you please join me at the head of the table. I believe you have earned the right to lead this company and these fine people."

After some very low-key celebration, followed by an early dinner we all left for our rooms for the evening. All, that is, except for Daddy and Sunny, who had already began planning the transition of power. I, for one, had had enough. Everything kept spinning around in my head – I felt like I knew what happened, but couldn't quite put it all together. There were clues there that we all had missed. I guess, being a mystery writer, I saw things that were right in front of us that the others didn't see…or maybe I was seeing things that weren't there at all.

# 24

## Fear before Love; Either before Hate

"Literature provides the road map; but God provides the road."
-Amiyah Dumas-Orwatt

"Thank you both for coming. Can I get you anything; coffee, tea, soda? Something to eat perhaps?" Iverson said as he greeted us at the front desk of police headquarters.

"Thank you, no. How can we be of help detectives?" Daddy said as Detective MacCallum approached.

"Let's go into one of our interrogation rooms, sit and go over what we have."

As we sat Iverson continued, "The forensic team, along with Detective MacCallum, has provided a great deal of insight as to what happened yesterday morning."

MacCallum added, "And Iverson's questioning of the witnesses has filled in much of the missing parts; but we do have a few missing pieces that you can help us with."

"Sure. We'll be glad to help in any way that we can. It was an awful thing to happen; and to such a lovely young lady; how tragic." I could see that Daddy genuinely felt that way about Joanna.

"Let's begin with what we know. We have a dead body – that of Joanna Leisner, who, according to the coroner died of blunt force trauma. The blow to the skull crushed the skull and she died almost immediately. The fall down the stairs broke her neck, but that was incidental – simply gravity doing its thing."

Then he began to go into great detail what they had as evidence, "We have a murder weapon – the bust of Diogenes on which we found the blood of the victim."

In a somewhat nervous gaff I interrupted, "How ironic. You do know that Diogenes was a man living in Ancient Greece who traveled throughout Athens looking for one honest man. And here we have a quite dishonest person using **his** bust to commit a dishonest act. I find that a bit unsettling, to say the least."

They all ignored my otherwise brilliant observation.

Iverson continued, "Yes, well; we have seven people who were together in a room just down the hall from where the murder took place, when it took place – all witnesses to each others innocence, or guilt for that matter."

Iverson listed the facts from his small pad, which he held in one hand as he flipped pages with the other.

"So far your list seems correct. Please continue," Daddy interjected.

"We have a darkened hallway with an open staircase that leads down exactly twenty-three stairs to the lower landing and a stone floor. We have a handkerchief with the initials A.D.O. embroidered on it which contains the victim's blood. And finally we have two people not in the room, and not with each other – our potential murder suspects. They are the aforementioned Mr. Odell and a Ms. Sunny Lanai. Am I missing anything?"

"I believe you have it all; that is, well, ah. Oh, no; never mind. Like I said; it is probably unimportant to your investigation," I said as Daddy flashed me a look of distain.

"Oh, Ada. Now here you go writing your mystery stories. 'The cook did it'; or 'the maid did it'; why not just say 'the butler did it'!" Daddy said in a very annoyed voice directed at me.

As we got up, shook hands and said the usual, 'if there is anything else that we can help with please feel free to call on us any time, day or night', Iverson lowered his head and put two fingers to his mouth and said, "Just one more little thing that's kind of bothering me folks. Maybe you could clear it up for me."

"Sure detective; anything," Daddy said.

"Well. It may be nothing, but on that handkerchief our team found three sets of prints – those of Alfonse, Sunny and another person we don't know. Of course it could be anyone that Alfonse had contact with since he washed it, but the prints didn't belong to anyone we interviewed at your house. Our team got all of your prints then. What do you think? Was there anyone else at the house? It would sure make it easier for us."

"Well, as I was about to say a moment ago there were two others in the house – Mrs. Higgins, our cook, and Clarissa, our housekeeper. But I'm sure they had no reason to harm any of our guests. In fact, Clarissa used to work for Henry and Joanna before she came to us; and Mrs. Higgins hardly knows any of the people we had staying at our house.

"Now folks; let's not second guess here. I'm sure you're probably right; but let's see if they had the means, motive and opportunity. It's our job to 'eliminate the impossible so that whatever is left, however improbable, has to be the answer' – as my childhood detective hero, Sherlock Holmes, used to say."

"You see what I have to work with," MacCallum added with a laugh.

We all felt the moment ease and joined with her and had a good laugh – even Iverson.

As they walked us to the front door Daddy stopped for a moment, turned to Iverson and posed a final question. He couldn't leave without getting some bit of inside information from the detectives. Daddy was used to being in the know.

"Detectives; you have been so kind to share what you have so far; I wonder if you couldn't go out a bit more and give us a hint as to who you suspect. Of course, anything you tell us will be held in the strictest confidence; I assure you."

I could see that, while MacCallum might be a rookie, Iverson has been in this game far too long to let out anything that might jeopardize the investigation.

"I'm sorry folks. I wish I could; but right now I need to think things through and lay out the evidence. You know; sort of mull it all over a bit. But you'll be the first to know; that is, after we apprehend the perp. And thanks again for coming down to the station today. We'll be in touch."

As we were leaving I could see Iverson taking a musty-looking old jacket off of a coat rack and head out the back door with his partner. I had to wonder how he ever solved a case.

# 25

## The Arrest

**"Sometimes ya gotta grab the bull by the balls if ya wanna get**
**his attention!"**
**-Slick**

"We're all here; but why? Did the police find the person who did it?" everyone was asking.

"Will everyone please take a seat. The detectives have just called and told me that they are on their way here. I know you are all wondering why you've been called here to take part in this most unusual situation. But I assure you that this is not a game; nor is it meant to intimidate you. Detectives Iverson and MacCallum have been gracious enough – and, I might add, in part due to my influence with the police commissioner – to indulge me by having you all participate in this, the conclusion to a horrible tragedy. A perpetrator has been identified and an arrest is immanent."

It's strange how people react. As Daddy announced this to the group gathered in the study at Ravenswood I could see several of them squirm. I don't think that it was because they were guilty, but more a matter of they probably had wished they had thought of doing it if they knew that Henry would step down. In fact, I believe Mariah would have killed all of them to get the position.

"As I speak…detectives, please come in and make yourselves at home."

"Thank you all for coming here this morning," Iverson began. "I know this is a bit unusual; it's a bit unusual for us as well. But this may actually work out for the benefit of all and put some closure on what appears to me to be a bit of an unusual case."

At that, MacCallum began going over all of the forensic findings, concluding with the prints on the handkerchief.

Iverson interrupted, "It was then that the sticking point hinged on a small clue that eluded us."

"Yes, the finger prints on the handkerchief," MacCallum jumped back in. "We found Alfonse's, which would seem natural since it belonged to him; Sunny's, when she explained that she found it laying on table near the fireplace, right over there." She pointed across the room as she spoke.

She continued, "After picking it up and examining it, she laid it back down thinking no more of it since Alfonse had sat in the chair next to that table earlier when he was so upset at finding Delmar passed out in the lower level; thus, her prints."

Iverson continued once more, "But the third set baffled us. They didn't belong to any of you that we had gotten prints from; but they did belong to someone who was in the house and who had motive, means and opportunity to kill Joanna. That's when we began to look deeper into the motive."

Daddy seemed to be enjoying this far too much. It was almost like a game to him; as if he had lost all sense that someone had actually died.

At this point I broke in, "I think it is time now to let down the charade. You all know deep down that you would feel no compunction about doing away with whomever to climb to the top. Daddy and I feel it vital in order for us to go on with our lives and our work that we make a clean slate of things. This will be painful and cathartic as well".

Daddy stood up and moved to the fireplace to get everyone's attention away from the detectives and me, where we stood opposite him at the entrance to the room.

"Sunny had opportunity, since her whereabouts when this happened are unaccounted for. She was the one who found Joanna and could have easily been the one to kill her. She is certainly strong enough to have lifted the bust of Diogenes and struck the blow that killed Joanna; and she was alone in this room where the handkerchief was last seen – thus providing her the means. She also had motive, as Henry was the primary threat to her gaining the head position at Orwatt Enterprises. However, as bad as it looks – she didn't do it. I believe, of all the members of this group, she genuinely liked Joanna and therefore would have killed Henry – or any of the rest of you for that matter – before she would have killed Joanna."

I felt the need to get into the dirt so I jumped in, "And dear, sweet Mariah, a real pariah when it comes to smelling the blood in the water. You couldn't have done it since, like Delmar, Robert, and Brent were in the room with most of the rest of us at the time of the murder. I also know that you are too focused on your little affair with Brent to even care about Joanna. If you were to kill anyone it would have been Sunny."

MacCallum spoke up sensing this becoming a witch hunt, "And finally, Alfonse; the only other member of this group who had motive, means and opportunity. His prints were on the handkerchief, he was alone at the time of the murder. His alibi, while it seems a bit feeble, saying that he was lost in the house, is actually very plausible. His motive would obviously have been to put Delmar in the top two for the position. But he also didn't do it."

Henry spoke up, "I'm not amused by this. The woman I loved was murdered and you're making a game of it!"

Daddy, feeling guilty for this whole situation, chimed in, "I am sorry. You're right. Detective please get to the point here so we can move on."

"Of course, Mr. Orwatt. What we found was there is someone else that had motive, means and opportunity to commit this crime. Clarissa Hodgeson you are under arrest for the murder of Joanna Leisner. You have the right…"

As Detective Iverson read her Miranda Rights Detective MacCallum put handcuffs on her and then led her away to the awaiting patrol car outside. We all sat there stunned until finally Iverson returned, alone, to relate the details that led up to Clarissa's arrest.

"I know you are all stunned by this; so let me explain how the details unfolded to us. We spoke yesterday with Mr. and Mrs. Orwatt down at the station. In our interview Mrs. Orwatt informed us that there were two others in the house at the time the murder took place – Mrs. Higgins, the cook, and Ms. Hodgeson, the housekeeper. Now Mrs. Higgins, while she can get around the kitchen pretty good as I understand, is not quite spry enough, nor strong enough to have committed the crime. Besides, she barely knew Joanna; so she had no motive, little means and not a whole lot of opportunity since she was busy all day in the kitchen."

This all made sense to the group; you could see by their expressions.

"But Ms. Hodgeson had all three – means, motive and opportunity. Let me explain. As you all know, Ms. Hodgeson has previously worked for Henry Palmer prior to, and shortly after, he and Ms. Leisner got together. It seems that Mr. Palmer's relationship with Ms. Hodgeson was more than just employee/employer and when Ms. Leisner moved in and discovered this – well, you know, one of them had to go. Guys, let me clue you in – they always find out."

A smile ran across MacCallum's face. She added, "And he should know."

Iverson flashed a look that spoke volumes as he interrupted her, "If I may continue? While Joanna was gracious enough to give her a good recommendation to the Orwatt's – probably an arrangement worked out amongst the three – there were bitter feelings between the two women. Ms. Hodgeson is certainly strong enough, and with the jealousy she probably had for Ms. Leisner she could have easily struck the blow that killed her. As the housekeeper, she had free access to any room here at Ravenswood Hall and it wouldn't appear at all strange for her to be in any particular place at any given time. I figure she saw the handkerchief with the initials A.D.O. and thought that it belonged to Ada and not Alfonse. No offense, but this handkerchief looks like one a woman, more than a man, would carry."

Alfonse jumped in, "None taken. You could have also taken notice that it smelled like lavender, my fav."

"I'm sure it does, but with all the blood on it I guess we missed the fragrance; sorry."

He continued, "Where was I? Oh, yes; she not only held a deep grudge against Joanna, she must have also hated Mrs. Orwatt as well. You see, how can I put this delicately?"

MacCallum rolled her eyes and said, "When have you ever put anything delicately. Just go on – please!"

"Well, I've found that the wealthy sometimes have a tendency to demean their help, especially the woman of the house. I'm sure unintentionally – of course."

"Of course," I shot back with an air of innocence. "I suspect this case is no exception," he added.

Seeing the look he was getting from the group, especially the women, Iverson moved on, "Needing a job to support herself and her elderly parents, Ms. Hodgeson allowed the two women – that is, Ms. Leisner and Mrs. Orwatt – to shuffle her around like a possession. She felt helpless in the matter, I'm sure. This created the hatred she had pent-up inside for the two of them. She saw her opportunity to eliminate Ms. Leisner, and thus opening up the possibility to get back with Henry – and the chance to get back at Mrs. Orwatt for all of her abuse. The perfect murder; and no one would suspect the housekeeper.

At this point I had to speak up, "I think I owe you an apology Detective Iverson."

"Why is that ma'am?" he responded quizzically.

"You see I mistook you for a bit of a fool. After our interview at the station yesterday I was amazed at how inept you appeared to be. I guess, being a mystery writer myself, I thought that the investigator had to be sharp and have all of the answers in order to solve a crime. I guess you've helped me change that attitude…and maybe my mysteries will improve dramatically with a character like you solving the crimes. Thank you."

Everyone could see a big grin break out on his face; he was (as they say in the south) in hog heaven!

"Thank you for that. I know I'm no Sherlock Holmes; but I do get the job done. Isn't that right MacCallum?" "Ugh…now he'll be impossible to live with!" she responded.

# 26

## Time to 'Fess Up'

**"'Nothing in life is ever easy; and if it is, you must have done it wrong!"
-Slick**

"So Hap; it's been what, three weeks and you never did tell us what grade you got on your story. You remember; when I was still in the hospital? We were all so caught up in your story we forgot about the grade; but I guess you planned it that way, didn't you – you sly dog? Well, what grade did you get?" Joanie still doesn't forget about details.

"Let's just say I'm graduating and leave it at that. Professor 'Heartless' didn't make it easy. But before I left he let me know that I had done well. I guess what Slick says is true."

"Don't tell me you're going to quote him," Joanie said with a half surprised look on her face.

That brought me back into reality. The stress of this whole project and her ordeal must be getting to me if I'm beginning to quote Slick. But what the heck?

"It's like he says, 'Nothing in life is ever easy; and if it is, you must have done it wrong!'"

She just rolled her eyes and threw a sofa pillow at me. Thank God we weren't sitting in our rock garden!

"Now how about us enjoying the rest of the day and go out to Wrightsville Beach and get some sun?"

"So you won't tell me your grade? That's okay I'm the one who gets the mail. I can wait until it comes then. Ha!"

I had to add, "We might as just as well be married; you're even reading my mail now. What if I had some honey on the side that sent me juicy love letters? What would you do then?"

"I guess I'd have to kill you. But I'd make you write out how I did it first! Ha, ha."

We had a good laugh, packed a few things and headed off for Johnny Mercer's Pier.

# Part IV: The Rest

A journey you've been taken on;
It has been most discrete.
With players who have served me well –
Their story is complete!

# 27

## Phase 2 – Part 1

**"As my friends south of the border say, 'When life gives you moles, make Móle!'"**
**-Slick**

"Slick, Slick, SLICK! You're as bad as Hap. Would you please get off the couch and find Susie. She needs to get a move on or I'll be late for my own wedding!"

"Alright, but this is my favorite episode of 'Road Runner'. This is where he…"

"I don't care! I've never cared. And if you don't turn that off right now and find Susie you'll need to be the Road Runner to keep me from beating you senseless. You get it?"

"Okay. Don't stroke out already. I'll find her. And why are you picking one me. Hap's right here watching it too."

"Now don't get ME into your fight. Just be happy you're not the one marrying her," I complained.

"I heard that. If you don't want to marry me; then that's fine. I won't…"

"Now Joanie; I was just kidding. Of course I want to marry you." Bad timing on my part.

"Why do they always hear what you don't want them to hear?"

Slick chuckled at that.

"And I heard that too!" she added.

"Slick, just get going would you, before I mess things up for good," I told him.

"Sure. But as my friends south of the border say, 'When life gives you moles, make Móle!'"

"You don't have any friends in Mexico; and besides that doesn't make any sense." Sometimes I forget who I'm talking to – when will I learn?

"I didn't say I had friends in Mexico. These are friends at the truck stop. You know – South of the Border – the one just off the I-95 on the way from North to South Carolina."

"Why do I bother?" I sighed.

"Here she is now. See if you just wait long enough it will come to you…in this case, she will." Slick sat there with his usual shit-eating grin wanting to tell us I told you so; but I think even **he** knew better than to do that.

"What? Was everyone waiting for me? I'm sorry; I had to redo my hair. I didn't like the way it looked."

I could see Joanie about to boil over as she turned toward Susie and responded, "You would think that this was your wedding and not mine!"

I thought, as dangerous as it might be, it would be best if someone got between the two of them before it broke out into a cat fight.

"I'm flattered to see that you both find me so irresistible, but I'm sorry – only one of you can have me."

That broke the tension. They both slowly broke into smiles; then they began to laugh and hug. Before I knew it the two of them, along with Slick, piled on me and began tickling me. I began to laugh as well.

After a few minutes of mayhem Joanie snapped back into reality, "Hey, we'd better be going. I know that this is not the Royal wedding, but we do have a priest, our families and a few friends waiting downtown at St. Mary's for us to show up."

So, we all piled into my old Olds-mo-Buick and headed downtown.

As we raced down Market Street still laughing and all chattering away Susie changed the happy mood with a very unsettling remark, "Isn't it bad luck for the groom to see the bride before the wedding?"

Joanie didn't make much of it. Her only comment on that was, "You make your own luck in life."

But that unnerved me a bit, and I could see that Slick felt the same way. Even though Joanie seemed to dismiss the remark, we all sat there silent for the remainder of the ride to the church.

As I drove, in my read-view mirror I could see a sinister smirk of satisfaction on Susie's face as she sat next to Slick in the back seat.

# 28

## A Girls Weekend

**"Just because you're paranoid doesn't mean everyone's not out to get you!"**
**-Hap**

"Joanie, Joanie, JOANIE!"

"What do you want; I'm right here? And why are you yelling?" Joanie replied to my calls.

"Nothing; I just wanted to see how it felt to do that. I can see why you do it; it feels kinda good."

Joanie shook her head and said, "I give up; you're hopeless. But fortunately for us both I'm going away for a long weekend with Susie and you can call out my name as much as you like. Won't that be fun?"

"I almost forgot. This is the weekend that you and Susie are going skiing at Snow Shoe in West Virginia, isn't it?"

"Well, how nice of you to remember; yes it is. We're leaving on Thursday so we can start skiing early Friday morning. We'll be back sometime late Sunday. We plan to ski at least half the day Sunday, so it will be very late when we get home; so don't wait up for us. I know how you worry, so I'll call by 11 in the evening to let you know where we are; but I really want you to go to bed and get some sleep."

"Not gonna happen, sorry. I won't be going to bed for two reasons. First, I can't help worrying about you and Susie driving home so late; and second, I have to have that story on 'Tourist Traps of the Southeastern Coast' done and in to the Star News by four in the morning – and I'll still be working on that right up until it's time to email it to the editor. So call me anytime, you won't wake me."

"I'll be fine; we'll be fine. Susie and I have skied since we were little kids. I know Kissing Bridge is no Snow Shoe, but we can handle these bigger hills. In fact, I'm planning to do some trail skiing; I just hope Susie is up for that."

"I just have one question," I asked. "What is it now? Boy I can't wait to go."

I heard her snide remark and said, "Was that necessary?"

"Alright, I'm sorry. What is your question?"

"What's today?"

*     *     *

Thursday came and went, as did Joanie and Susie – on their way to their skiing weekend. Slick and I decided to hang out at my place for the weekend; sort of a bachelor pad for a few days. No big plans; just watch some TV, drink some beer and order out. I knew that Joanie and Susie were both competent skiers because we all (including Slick) used to ski almost every weekend in the winter back home in Buffalo – and winter there meant from November until April some years!

*     *     *

"Hap, how do you think the girls are getting along? I'll bet they are miserable without us."

"Slick; are you dreaming? Are we miserable without them right now?" I said in wonderment at his comment.

"No, but don't forget we have 'Road Runner' and 'Rocky and Bullwinkle' and they don't have a TV where they're staying."

I knew better than to be logical with him so I replied, "Of course, how could I forget."

He just beamed with satisfaction thinking that he was smarter than me. I just let him delude himself.

*     *     *

Everything was fairly quiet, that is, until Saturday night. It was almost 10 p.m. when my phone rang; it was Susie. She

~ 168 ~

sounded in a panic. I could hardly understand what she was trying to tell me.

"Hap, It's Joanie. There's been a terrible accident. I'm at the hospital now. The doctors are concerned. You've got to come... Now!"

"Susie, slow down. Who's hurt? Is it Joanie? What happened? Take a deep breath and start over."

"It's Joanie. She ran into a big tree on one of the trails. We were on Shay's Revenge, a double black diamond trail. I told her that we should start off on an easier trail, like Powder Monkey; but she insisted. She said anything less than a black diamond trail wasn't worth our time on the lift." Susie paused to catch her breath.

After a moment she began again with, "The slopes were icy from the changes in temperature; it had been warm during the day, but now, as night was falling, it was beginning to get pretty cold. I tried to warn her, but she caught a patch of ice as we were winding down the lower part of the trail. I was following her at the time, but just as she was turning to follow the curve in the trail someone skied passed me and hit the same icy snow that Joanie was slipping on, and ran into her - hard. When that happened it sent Joanie flying uncontrollably into a big pine tree." "Did the other skier stop to help? What happened?" I said in a panicked tone.

"It happened so fast, and there was a lot of powder flying. I couldn't see the other skier's face; and before I could do anything, he or she was gone."

"What! How is she? Where are you now?" I couldn't believe what I was hearing. Slick heard my frantic voice and came running into the kitchen where I sat at the bar on the phone with Susie.

"Hap, what is it? Has someone gotten hurt?" he asked.

"Shh, I'm trying to find out right now. Susie, are you still there?"

"Yes Hap. Right after I got to her a man who was coming down the trail stopped, saw her lying there and told me to stay with her; he would get help. The ski patrol came right away with a stretcher, an oxygen tank and some other medical supplies. I could see that she was in pain and that she probably had several broken bones. She kept slipping in and out of consciousness...Oh Hap; you got to get here right away!"

"What's the name of the hospital and what town are you in?"

After Susie gave us the information Slick and I grabbed a few things and headed out the door and into the car. Off we raced to Snow Shoe, West Virginia.

\*       \*       \*

It was early Sunday morning by the time we arrived at Davis Memorial Hospital in Elkins, West Virginia. We found Susie in the ICU waiting room, sleeping on a small couch. She was curled up in a ball with her right arm hanging over the edge and a coffee cup dangling precariously from her fingers.

"Susie, Susie. Wake up; it's morning. Hey, how is she?"

As she began to come around she opened her eyes and wiped off the drool that was running down her cheek and said, "Hap, Slick; you made it! How was your ride here?"

Slick and I just looked at each other. I could see that he was thinking the same thing, that that was an odd thing to say; but I chalked it up to her just waking up.

"Ah, the ride was okay; we flew here as fast as Slick's old car would go. How's Joanie; where is she right now? I've got to talk to the doctors, or nurses, or someone."

By this time she was fully awake and sitting up. She took my arm and said, "Sit down a minute. I'll take you to where she is, but first you need to get a hold of yourself."

Slick saw my panic and said, "Yeh, Hap. Slow down. She's alright; isn't she Susie?"

Susie responded, "She's pretty banged up, but she's going to be okay."

"I knew that this trip was a bad idea. I shouldn't have let her come without me. This never would have happened if I were here; I wouldn't have let her ski those trails with the icy conditions."

Slick and Susie could see that I was over-thinking this whole thing. They could probably tell that I was going over every thing I've done wrong; every little cross word or insensitive action directed at Joanie over the years – and regretting every one of them. It's funny how we do things to others, even those we love, that we don't give a second thought to until it's too late. Then we regret it the rest of our lives. I guess it's part of human nature; I guess it's part of what our conscience is all about. Not to mention that Catholic and Italian guilt thing that I have going for me. Life was just getting easier for us. After only six years of marriage we were finally in the place in life we had hoped to be; and we were talking about having a family.

Slick broke the silence and brought me back into reality.

"Hap, I want to tell you a story. It's about Sarge. Maybe this will help make some sense of things."

"Slick. I'm not in the mood for one of your stupid family stories. I'm not in the mood for humor; no matter how well intended."

"No Hap. This isn't a funny story. It's about the time, the only time, I ever saw Sarge cry. It happened when my mom died a few years back. You remember; you were all there for me. Well, after the funeral I took Sarge for a little ride to Chestnut Ridge Park in Orchard Park. I thought that, since it was a cool, sunny day in Buffalo, I might cheer him up a little. Don't get me wrong, I felt the pain of my mother dying too, but it seemed to hit Sarge like a sledge hammer. I've never seen anything affect him this way."

I lost all thought of the moment and drifted back to that day and tried to visualize their ride through the park – remembering our own times there together as teenagers.

"We talked about old times with mom; you know, as everyone does to remember the person when they were alive; the happy moments. As I was remembering one of those times Sarge interrupted me, as if he hadn't heard a word of what I was saying."

"You know, when your mother and I met I had just come home from Ft. Dix and had been discharged from the Army. I saw her at the Hens and Kelly Department Store in downtown Buffalo. Ah, she was a sight; there behind the register in the men's department. I needed some new civilian clothes now that I was back home. When I saw her she seemed to glow. It was Christmas 1947 and the store was packed with holiday shoppers; but she stood out from everyone around her. As she looked up from the counter where she was ringing up a sale our eyes met and everyone else seemed to melt into the shadows. We must have stared at one another a good long while because the customer that she had been waiting on began to wave her hand in front of your mother's face as if to bring her out of a trance. And for my part my buddy, Herb that I was shopping with, gave me an elbow in the ribs to bring me around."

"At this he began to cry and sob. He never did finish his story...or maybe he did. I don't know; but one thing I do know is that when you love someone like that – like you love Joanie – it doesn't matter what you would like to change, or what you've said or done in the past that you regret. What matters is what you have together. And just like Sarge and Lulu, you two have the kind of relationship most other people only wish for."

At that, he put his arm around my shoulder and pulled me to himself. We sat for a while like that until Susie broke the silence with an announcement.

"Let's go see if we can get one of the doctors to talk with you."

Susie led Slick and me down a long hall and into another waiting area where there was a nurses' station. It was just about six in the morning and we had to wait for a nurse to come to the desk.

"Can I help you?" she asked looking from one of us to the other waiting for a response.

I spoke up, "Yes I'm here to see Joanie Pozner. I'm her husband, and these are our friends. Can I go in to see her, and is there a doctor around that can tell me about her condition?"

"Let me get Dr. Powers. He is the doctor who was on duty last night; he is about to finish his shift this morning, so let me go and catch him before he leaves. He was the doctor who saw your wife last night when she came in to the emergency room. Wait right here; I'll be back in a few moments," she directed as she rushed away to find the attending doctor.

As we stood there for, what seemed like forever, I couldn't help wondering how many people are admitted to this hospital that are involved in skiing accidents. Being one of the area hospitals around a big ski resort I thought that they must see skiers just about every day during the skiing season. Somehow that thought came as a consolation to me; that is, knowing that they take care of people in Joanie's condition all the time. They've had a lot of practice and that should mean that she was in good hands. I only hope she will be okay.

"Hap, are you alright?" Slick said.

I could see a worried look on his face; I think he was more worried right now about me than he was about Joanie.

"Sure Slick. I'm just worried about how she is."

"Well, don't over-think this. Wait until we get to see her. She's probably not as bad as you might imagine. You know how you get sometimes," Slick replied.

"I guess you're right, but I wish that nurse would hurry up and get here with the doctor so we could find out – and get to see her."

"Hap, I was with her right up until they took her in for x-rays last night. She was conscious and seemed to be holding up pretty good; and I'm sure once they gave her something for the pain she was able to relax and maybe even sleep a little…Look, here comes Dr. Powers now, with the nurse."

"Mr. Pozner, I'm Dr. Powers. I was the physician who saw your wife last night when she came into the emergency room," he said as he shook my hand and greeted me with a smile. I took that to be a good sign.

"Hello doctor. These are our friends Susie and Slick. I guess you probably met Susie last night…"

As I was rambling on with my introductions, he interrupted me with, "Well, I'm sure you would like to see her as soon as possible."

I caught myself and replied, "Of course. Sorry for the rambling there; we drove all night to get here and I guess I'm a bit tired."

"That's quite alright. Now I would like to go over her condition with you before we go in there. Don't worry, she's resting quite comfortably now. The nurse has gone in to wake her and tell her that you're here, so we have a few minutes to talk first."

"Sure."

"Do you mind if your friends wait here for you; I'd like to talk with you – alone."

I looked at Susie and Slick and said, "Doctor, these are our closest friends. I think that they should hear about her condition as well; after all, I going to force them to help me get her back into shape once we get home."

They all chuckled a bit at my remark. I guess my nervousness about hearing how she was made me a little off balance.

"Mr. Pozner…"

I interrupted with, "Please call me Hap."

"Hap, your wife has suffered severe trauma from her accident. Not only was there the force from her hitting the tree at a high speed; add to that someone, who was moving faster than her hitting her and catapulting her, so to speak, into it. That caused her to strike it with an even greater force."

"What exactly are you saying doctor?" I interjected.

"Well, what I'm getting at is because of the force of her encounter with the tree she has suffered quite a few injuries. She has broken five ribs, her right wrist; her right hand and forearm are fractured. She also suffered injuries to her left leg and foot. She must have twisted her left leg under her because she has broken her left ankle and fractured her tibia, as well as severely bruising her left hip; and she has a concussion as well. Now I know this sounds very bad, but the good news, if we can say there is any, is that there doesn't appear to be any internal injuries to any vital organs – and that is wonderful news. You have no idea of how many people we see who come here having suffered the same kind of skiing accident who are much worse off than your wife is."

"So this is good news?" I was confused.

"Well, I guess you could say it is as good as it could be given the accident she was in," he responded.

After a short silence he began again.

"Fortunately for her she seems to have kept herself in good physical condition and she is young. These are the things, besides her strong will to live, and quick reaction avoiding a direct contact to the tree with her head, that will help her recover. She should make an almost complete recovery from her injuries."

"Excuse me doctor," Susie interrupted. "You said 'an almost complete recovery'. What do you mean by that?"

"Well, of course, she will have to have physical therapy to strengthen her arms and leg once the bones are healed; but she may, to one degree or another, have anywhere from a slight limp to...well, I hate to say this possibility..."

"Don't hold any punches, doctor I need to know," I said. "Of course; worst case scenario, she might need to walk with a cane, depending on how her left leg heals. That's where she sustained the worst of her injuries as I talked about a moment ago."

"Now I think it might be good for you, as well as Joanie, if you go in to see her," he said, trying to get my mind off what he had just told us.

As I got up to leave Susie and Slick I could see that Susie had a troubled look on her face.

"Are you alright, Susie?" I asked.

"Sure Hap. I'm fine. I was just thinking; that's all. You go see Joanie – and send her our love. Slick and I will take a walk down to the café and get some coffee and something to eat. We'll bring something back for you. What would you like?"

"What? Eat food from a hospital café. You know café is short for caf-e-ter-ia, don't you? And did you forget what our school cafeteria food tasted like? No thanks. I'd rather live; but I will take a cup of coffee."

"Sure. How do you like it?" Susie asked.

Before I could answer Slick responded with, "Like he likes his women, right Hap."

Susie fell into his trap, "Oh, how's that?'"

With a silly grin on his face already he said, "Bitter! Ha, ha."

"Oh, let's go. You're wasting everyone's time with your stupid remarks. I don't know why I even talk to you…"

I could hear her continue to scold him as they disappeared down the long hall. Just before fading out of sight I saw Slick turn his head toward me and shoot me a smile. Somehow that made me feel that everything was going to be alright again soon.

As Dr. Powers led me down the hall he began to give me some instructions.

"Don't look surprised when you see her. She has some minor scrapes and scratches on her face and neck as well; from hitting the tree. She must have been able to avoid hitting her head directly, though; because if she had, she would probably not be here with us today. Now she will have to be here a few days, but I think we will be able to release her to go home by Wednesday. I know you and your friends will probably want to stay in the area, so I've asked nurse Osborne to give you information on places in the area where you might be able to find lodging."

Still trying to sift through all of the information I just got, I replied, "Thank you doctor."

"Now, how about we go see that lovely bride of yours? Remember; she's going to want to see a big smile. Oh, by the way, be gentle – she's a bit tender right now. Also, it would be best if you sat on her left side if you're going to hold her hand. She struck the tree from her right; that's why most of the injuries were on that side."

"Got it; I'm ready."

As the two of us entered the room where Joanie was lying, the nurse was just finishing up with her. Dr. Powers greeted Joanie with a big smile and said, "Well, it's good to see our patient awake and in good spirits. You gave us quite a scare last night. Didn't anybody ever tell you that you should go around the trees?"

She gave a weak laugh and replied, "I figured that I could take it; but I guess it was just a little bit bigger than me."

"I have a visitor for you. Do you feel up to seeing him? I hear he came a long way to see you."

Just as he was saying this I came in from behind him at the doorway. It was so good to see her alive. Susie and Slick were still down at the café getting food and coffee.

"Well stranger; I always said I was a better skier than you. Obviously you can't handle a little icy turn," I chided, hoping to see the Joanie I knew.

And she showed it when she replied, "Oh, yeh mister? I handled the ice and turns. If it weren't for some idiot running in to me I would have never hit that tree. You know that I'm a MUCH better skier than you – any day. In fact, let's go right now. Get the nurse and have her unplug me. I'll show you."

We both began to laugh at her remark. My laughter turned to tears of joy, knowing that she was going to be okay.

"Don't ever do that again; please?" I said as I leaned over her and hugged her.

"Ow; are you trying to kill me!"

"I'm sorry." I sat back in the chair next to her and held her hand – gently.

"Now what are you doing taking on the hardest slopes first?" I asked.

"You know me Hap; I'm pretty cautious. I wanted to ski Powder Monkey for a while first, but Susie teased me about it. She reminded me that we were both excellent skiers and that we only had a couple of days to ski. I guess I let her talk me into it; but as you always say, 'No one can make you do anything that you don't want to unless you let them'. And you're right; I guess I really was anxious myself to hit the toughest trails. Although I didn't mean that I wanted to hit them literally!"

That stunned me. Joanie never lies, while Susie almost always does. But this was not just a little lie to get her way; this was a lie that could have cost Joanie her life. Why did Susie tell me it happened differently than Joanie?

I thought about how she said the accident happened and how Susie had told Slick and I earlier, and the two didn't seem to mesh at all; but this was not the time to bring it up. I needed to think it over and wait until Joanie was better and home with me before I started speculating. They were both in a situation that happened very fast and their adrenalin was flowing; so maybe what happened in reality was somewhere between the two stories. Besides, I know what she would say; she would quote one of my favorite expressions, 'Just because you're paranoid doesn't mean everyone's not out to get you!' and maybe I am a bit too paranoid about Susie; but I swear there's something to it.

After those few minutes alone, I called Susie and Slick into the room. They had stayed just outside the door after they got back with the food and coffee, to give me time to see her alone. We all talked and laughed a little. I didn't mention anything about the accident, if it was one!

Just as Dr. Powers had said, we were able to bring Joanie home on Wednesday. For the next several months I took care of my patient. It's a good thing that I can work from home. That is one advantage of being a freelance writer. I can email my articles and stories to various magazines and newspapers and still be here to help her every day. But she did get a bit crabby having to sit and lie down most of the time while she had her casts on; but Susie and Slick came over often to amuse her – and me.

* * *

It took more than six months between the healing process and follow up therapy, not to mention Joanie pushing herself, before she was able to do most of the things that she could before the accident. She still had some headaches from the concussion, and stiffness in her left leg, which made her walk with a limp. At first she had to use a cane, which she absolutely hated; but slowly her leg got better and she could walk without the cane.

# 29

## Life – the Other Option

**"It ain't a hangin' 'till the fat lady swings!"**
**-Slick**

"Hap, Hap, HAP! Hurry up. It's time to leave. I have a 10 o'clock doctor's appointment and it's quarter 'till. You can't be late for these or they'll make you wait forever."

"They make you wait forever anyway. Even if you get there on time you have to fill out a ton of paperwork, although they already have the information in their computer. Then when you're on about page nine or 10 of the form they call you in. So then they give you a nasty look when you hand them the clipboard and tell them that you didn't have time to finish it. Or they'll say something like, 'And people say we make them sit around waiting too long, hmm.'"

"Hap…"

"And then they weigh you, check your height, take your temperature and blood pressure; and you still haven't seen the doctor..."

"Hap, would you please..."

"Finally, they put you in a room where you...come on...you know...that's right; THEY MAKE YOU WAIT SOME MORE!"

"HAP, WOULD YOU PLEASE STOP!"

"Okay, I'm done ranting."

"No. I mean stop the car. I forgot my coffee cup. It's on top of the car!"

As I brought the car to a screeching halt we saw the cup slide down the front windshield, hit the wiper blade, fall on its side spilling its contents all over the front hood, and roll off the edge of the right front fender. This dance down the car was followed by the sound of the cup breaking when it hit the pavement. We looked through the windshield at the remnants of the coffee, then at each other.

She said, "Let's go." I nodded; and back on our way we went.

I wasn't sure how to approach the subject, but something was bothering me. It was like I had been putting the pieces of a puzzle together for years and didn't quite have all the pieces in place yet – and couldn't tell what the picture was.

"Joanie, I'd like to talk to you about something that's been eating at me for some time now."

"Oh, here we go. Is this going to be one of your stories; because, if it is, I don't have time right now to listen. Remember…we're on our way to the doctor for me to have more tests done."

"I know, I know. No; this isn't one of my stories. It's about you…you and Susie I mean."

"What about Susie and me?"

"Well, do you remember when you fell down the stairs that night at Poplar Grove Plantation when we were re-enacting my murder mystery?"

"Yes. But what's that got to do with anything?"

"And do you remember what you said when I asked how it happened. You said you felt a hand on your shoulder shove you toward the stairs and then Susie grabbing your hand to stop you from falling."

"Of course I remember. Who would forget something like that. I hit my head on the way down and was in a coma for the next few weeks for God's sake; how could I forget! Oh, I know. You're not going to let me forget how you nagged me to take it easy for the next two years. What's your point?"

"Okay. Let's go back even further; back to grade school. Do you remember how Susie had to win at everything and how it was because of her mother pushing her all the time. In fact, to the point that Susie, after telling us all about her mom and about her horrible experience with Mr. Sweeney, she finally cracked and tried to commit suicide."

"What are you getting at Hap? You're beginning to scare me."

"When we were young Susie and I seemed to always compete for the prize. First the cello, then the spelling bee, next the essay contest, not to mention the Valedictorian award, and on and on. And she always won; that is, until she told me about what Mr. Sweeney was doing and Slick and I started to harass him with the phone calls. You remember I took a beating for her; but, with the help of my Uncle Sallie, he left town. After that she stopped trying to beat me at everything. In fact, I kind of felt like she began to like me a little too much. You know what I mean. She seemed to treat me different – kind of fixated on me."

Joanie laughed and added, "You mean she fell deeply, hopelessly, helplessly in love with you. Give me a break."

"No I'm serious now. Didn't you notice that after you and I became more than friends she started to become competitive with you. Didn't you see the look on her face when we were sitting around the campfire at Zoar Valley the night of our graduation; or the look she gave in the hospital, just after you came out of your coma, when I thanked her for saving your life that night at Poplar Grove."

"Okay. So maybe I'm thick; what are you telling me? That she's jealous that I've got you and all she has to look forward to is Slick? Well, guess what…you're comparing apples to coconuts! I love Slick; but he's not someone I'd ever marry – or date for that matter. Hell, I'd become a nun first. You're giving yourself much too much credit in the sex appeal department, no offense."

"None taken. No I'm not talking about a normal jealousy. Keep in mind the history I just laid out. I love Susie, but I don't think she's over the trauma she's had in her life; and I think it's screwing up how she thinks. Did you forget that she tried to kill herself once; or that she was in rehabilitation for some time after that?"

"Alright; let's say, for the time being, that you're on to something. What exactly are you on to?" Joanie looked more confused than when I started this whole conversation.

"Okay, but before I continue with that line of thought, let me throw in something more recent. You just went skiing with her and had an 'accident'. I call it that because I can't prove different. You told me that you were doing fine on the trail, even with the ice. According to you, you would have never hit that big tree if it weren't for someone slamming into you causing you to lose your balance, right?"

"Yeh. So what's your point?"

"Well, according to what Susie told Slick and me over the phone, you had slipped on the icy patch and then someone ran into you causing you to hit the tree! Doesn't that strike you as odd?"

"Hap; you're making too much of this. So, maybe she thought that I was slipping on the ice. Maybe from her perspective it looked like I was. What's the difference? What are you getting at?"

"What I'm getting at is, what if she was the 'unknown skier' that ran into you – on purpose that night on the slope, and what if she not only was the person who grabbed your hand to save you, but she was also the person who pushed you that night at Poplar Grove?"

Joanie interrupted, "Slow down cowboy! I'll give you, maybe she was a bit jealous over our relationship, but to try to kill me – twice? That's a bit of a stretch. So let me get this straight, she first tries to kill me at Poplar Grove Plantation, but then a second later – after she has no time to think it over – decides to save me out of guilt. Then, not being satisfied, she tries again six years later when we're on a skiing trip together at Snow Shoe. Doesn't that sound a touch beyond your normal paranoia?"

"Maybe you're right. But I still don't feel settled about this whole thing."

"Look it. We're here; can we get out of the car and get this over with. Susie is what she is…and by the way Slick is no prize either. But they're our good friends. So be happy…P-L-E-A-S-E?"

"Okay. I'll let it go for now. But I'm not satisfied with the answers, and as Slick says, 'It ain't a hangin' 'till the fat lady swings!' Now, how about you buy me a cup of coffee after we get out of here?" To which she slugged me in the arm. She hasn't changed much in all of these years…that's what I love about her.

But I'll probably be black and blue there tomorrow.

# 30

## The Murder

"Some must die so that others may live."
-Unknown

"Hap, Hap, HAP!"

Once again I've been summoned from my own reality to one that everyone else shares – and I hate it.

"Yes. I'm busy. I'm finally getting some of my poems to where I'm beginning to like them."

I do enjoy these few precious moments I have alone to think and write. It's too bad no one else seems to think that what I do takes focus. I guess I'll just have to enjoy them as they come and stop trying to explain them to others. I shouldn't complain; what little time I am afforded it is much better than working for a living. I've had enough 'shit' jobs to know that. And who knows, maybe when I really start making money at it they'll begin to respect my time more. Oh, well.

\*       \*       \*

## Moments Alone

I cherish these moments,
The ones by myself;
My head spinning backwards,
Put life on a shelf.

As thoughts lead me nowhere,
They all serve me well;
If life will just let me,
My thoughts I can sell.

These wonderful seconds,
As hours I hone;
With words filled with feeling,
In moments alone.

\*       \*       \*

"I'M NOT GOING TO TELL YOU AGAIN…DO YOU HEAR ME!"

WHAT IS IT, NOW?" Why is everyone always so dramatic – sheesh.

"Come downstairs – NOW! Slick and Susie are here. You need to come down and hear what's happened."

~ 190 ~

Joanie's voice had a sense of urgency in it, along with a panic that alarmed me. I jumped up from my work and raced to the kitchen where the three of them were sitting around the table
– staring silently at me as I came through the doorway.

With a smile that quickly melted away and became a look of fear I said, "What is it?"

"Sit down Hap. We've got some very bad news."

"I'm here. What's happened? Are you guys alright? Is this some sort of a joke you're trying to pull on me?" I was noticeably confused by their demeanor.

"This is serious Hap," Joanie interrupted. Then

Slick spoke up, "Hap, Devon is dead!"

At that Susie broke down and began to cry. Joanie moved over to her side and held her close as Slick went on.

"I found him when I came home from work to get changed and pick Susie up. I still had some clothes over at Devon's apartment from when I lived there, before Susie and I moved in together. Well, anyway, I went there to get a jacket I wanted to wear out tonight. Susie and I were supposed to be going out to a movie and dinner. When I got there I found the door to the apartment unlocked; I thought that that was a bit strange, but didn't make too much of it until – until I went in and looked around for my jacket. As I passed Devon's room I saw that his door was open a bit. I could see into the room enough to see him lying on the bed. At first I thought that he was just crashing for a while. You know how he likes to take his
'afternoon siestas' as he calls them. I knocked on the door and called his name, but he didn't answer. He didn't even move. So I

~ 191 ~

decided to go in. I didn't want him to wake up and hear me rooting around the apartment for my jacket and think that I was a prowler or something."

Slick paused to get his breath. We could hear the stress he must have been feeling as he relived this horrible event.

"When I went over to him I saw that he had been playing some sort of card game. A deck of cards were spread out on the bed next to him; and there was some drug paraphernalia lying on the night stand next to his bed, which seemed pretty odd to me. This was not just some grass, it was white powder and crystals. I went over to him and shook him, calling his name, but he didn't respond. His body was limp and cold. It was then I checked for a pulse and to see if he was breathing; he wasn't. I grabbed the phone and called for help. The ambulance and police were there in a few minutes. When they got there they rushed me out and into a waiting patrol car and began to question me about what I had found. Before I knew it the place was crawling with cops. After they questioned me they let me go and I tried to get back into the apartment, but by then they had taped off the doorway to the apartment and wouldn't let me back in."

Slick stopped to catch his breath again. He was hyperventilating from being so upset by this.

"What did you find out?" I shot back at him. I was anxious to find out just what had happened to our good friend.

"Well, after they questioned me and saw that I didn't kill my friend, they told me that it looked like he had died from an overdose. They said the stuff I found there was more than likely crack cocaine; but they would have the lab confirm it. He died from something I know he never did!"

"Wait a minute," Joanie snapped. "You're telling us that Devon did hard drugs? That's crazy!"

"I know. That's what I told them."

"What else did they say? What are they going to do?" Joanie was just as confused and surprised at this as we all were.

"They didn't say anything more; except that they would let me know what their investigation uncovers – of course, after they've talked to his family."

"Have you talked to them yet?" I asked.

"No. I thought that you all would want to do that with me."

And he was right. After we went down to the police station and talked with them we drove over to Devon's mom's house where his two brothers and three sisters were gathered with their families. It brought back memories of my father's death and how it left us. As we sat there with his family I kept hearing the same words, as if they were coming from Devon, telling me to write it down for him. It later became the poem I wrote for him and read at his funeral service.

*     *     *

## We are All the Same, Aren't We?

Wracked with pain of one loved lost-
The price of living, what life has cost.

When family, friend or stranger dies-
They stretch up through eternal skies.

For us to know, to understand-
Their life, their death – ours close at hand.

Of what we are or what he was-
With memories, thoughts or lack there of.

\*     \*     \*

# 31

## The King of Clubs

**"It's like Sarge always said, 'With great wealth comes great privilege!'"**
**-Slick**

Slick had just come over for his usual Saturday 'cartoon- fest' as he calls it. I call it wasting my morning; but then again, what are friends for, right?

"Slick, it's been more than three weeks now. Have you heard anything at all from the police?"

"No. But I'll tell you, that cop in charge of the investigation is one piece of work!"

I just ignored his remark and said, "Have you talked to Devon's family at all?"

"Yeh, I talked to his mom yesterday. I go to visit her a couple of times a week. She told me that the coroner declared it an accidental death. Now that guy would slip and slide in his own shit if it weren't for Igor, his assistant."

"Enough of the commentary; what did he say?"

"The coroner said that Devon overdosed and there was no evidence of fowl play. The police are still looking for where he got the stuff, though. They even called me in last week to see if I knew anything, or had anything, to do with his drug habit. Drug habit! Imagine that. He never did more than smoke up a bit, or drink beer or wine. They're crazy!" Slick responded, just as miffed as I was.

"Well I don't buy it either. In fact, I'm sure that there was some fowl play. But you lived with him, and we were almost always together; you know, the bunch of us. So where would he have gotten the stuff without us knowing about it? It's like he was leading a double life. It doesn't make sense."

"According to the police report Devon had enough drugs around the apartment to feed a small army. Now where would he get the money to buy all of that?" Slick queried.

I could see his brain going. You could almost see the smoke coming out of his ears – he was thinking so hard.

In his usual sarcastic way Slick added, "Well I guess he was filthy rich and we all just didn't know it, right? It's like Sarge always said, 'With great wealth comes great privilege!'"

Getting us back on track I said, "I don't think that Devon had the money or the interest in that stuff."

"I don't either. Other than the evidence, which the police took away, there was nothing different or unusual about the apartment."

"Think Slick. Was there any little thing that might help us out?"

"At first I didn't recall seeing anything that I thought was unusual, but when the police questioned me they asked me one question that reminded me of something that I did see that I thought was odd."

I could see his brain going again, "Well what was it?" "They asked me if Devon gambled. It was then that I remembered the deck of cards spread out on the bed next to him. When I saw it I was so worried about Devon I didn't make much of it, but when the cops asked about it I began to think that there was something strange about it. The cards weren't laid out like he was playing solitaire, or some game; it looked more like he was doing a card trick with them. That seemed very strange to me; Devon never did card tricks as long as I've known him. They were on the bed next to him fanned out in a semi-circle face down – all except the King of Clubs, which was laying face up in the middle of the circle."

"What do you suppose that means? Did you tell the detective that?"

"Of course I did. He just dismissed it. He said that it probably meant nothing; Devon might have been just messing with the cards as he was lulled into his euphoric state and then on into a coma and death. He told me that there was probably a lot that I didn't know about him, just as there was probably a lot he didn't know about me. And I guess he was right about that. So I didn't think much more of it."

I began to see red, "Slick; how could you dismiss the life of a good friend so easily? Would you do that if it were me? Look it, this must mean something. It must be a clue for us; but what?"

Slick could see that I was grasping at straws.

"Hap, I loved him just like the rest of you did, but I think that the detective might have been right. We don't know everything about everyone. Don't you remember Susie and her near death experience overdosing on her mother's pills? Well, we didn't see that one coming either; and we knew her much better – and much longer than we've known Devon. So come on, don't make this worse for us than it is. For that matter, don't make it worse for his family than it is, for God's sake!"

I could see his point, but I was sure there was a message Devon or someone was giving us. So I couldn't let it go.

Just then we heard Susie and Joanie laughing, coming up the front porch stairs to our house.

"Alright, we'll continue this later. I don't want the girls to get involved in what you and I are going to do right now. Okay?"

"Wait a minute. What is it that WE are going to do?"

Just then the door opened and in they walked with their arms full of grocery bags.

"Well, don't just sit there you two. Give Susie and I a hand with the groceries. And there's more in the trunk of the car. Hurry some of it might melt – and I know how you hate melted Rocky Road."

With that Slick jumped up, "Did someone say the magic words? Come on Hap; let's not keep these two beautiful ladies standing holding the bag – so to speak. Ha!"

"Just what have you two boys been up to? No good I'm sure," Susie added.

Slick just smiled as I started to squirm a little. I could never keep a poker face when I was trying to keep a secret.

I just said, "Ah, nothing; nothing at all. I'd better get out to the car to get that ice cream before it melts."

At that Slick just couldn't let the moment pass quietly. He began, "It's like I always say…"

Just as he was about to wax philosophical the three of us said in unison, "SHUT UP!"

"Okay; okay. No reason to get excited," he responded. We could hear him as he went out the door, "Such high strung people I have to put up with…sheesh!"

# 32

## Searching for Answers

**"It's the little things in life; they're the things that make it impossible to get anything done!"**
**-Slick**

Devon's death didn't set well with me. He didn't take drugs; at least not hard drugs. He never would have done anything so dangerous; and if he did — why would he be playing cards? It didn't make sense at all. And I know, even though he wouldn't talk about it, Slick thought the same way about it.

"Are you ready now to talk about Devon and how he died? I'll tell you — with or without you, I'm going to find out what really happened. You know me. I won't give up until I do."

"I know, I know. After all, I've put up with your OCD most of my life, haven't I?"

"Me? O.C.D.! That's a good one. I can't help it if I can focus well on something; okay, hyper-focus. Alright, maybe I am a bit OCD, but it does come in handy now and then. Now are you going to help me or not?"

Slick just shook his head and said, "Of course; you knew I would. Do I ever really have a choice? You just had to wear me down first, didn't you? Okay; what did you have in mind? What's our first move?"

We both smiled.

"As I've always said, 'It's the little things in life; they're the things that make it impossible to get anything done!'"

"So let's talk about where we need to begin," I had to get Slick back on track (again). Sometimes he has an uncanny way of discovering things that no one else can see.

"The first thing we need to do is to look at all of the possibilities and eliminate those that are impossible. This may not be something that was from his present life; after all we've know him these past five or six years – and haven't seen him with anyone that might be dangerous. What do we know about his past? Let's start there, okay?" Slick began to work his magic.

I added, "You may have something. Let's start with his family for clues; but let's not let them know the real reason we're looking into his past. Let's tell them we're writing a memoir or something like that. How does that sound?"

"That makes sense to me; but what about the girls?"

"I'm glad you brought them up. Say nothing to them – understood. They would just think it was my imagination; a story."

Slick understood clearly what I meant; and he didn't want any interference from them either.

So we sat down and jotted notes on what we knew about Devon and his past life. We called on his brothers and sisters to find out what they could tell us. We just told them we were writing a memoir of his life – sort of our tribute to him. They thought it was sweet. But it was his mother, surprisingly, who gave us our first clue; the link to what may have happened to

Devon.

"Mrs. Williams, I know this is painful for you, but we were Devon's best friends and we wanted to do something for his memory." I hated myself for lying to her, but I knew that it was for a greater good – so Devon could rest in peace; so we could be at peace as well.

"Son, there was a time when that young'un gave me a fit. You know with his different lifestyle and all. But even with that he was an angry young man. I s'pose 'cause of all the abuse he got from classmates about his being…well, you know. I remember a time he felt he had to get away or he'd bust, so I told him I'd arrange for him to go stay with my brother Harry who lives on the East Side of Buffalo, New York; over on Peach Street, just on the edge of the downtown area."

"That's something!" Slick interrupted. "He mentioned that he was from Buffalo, but his family moved to Wilmington when he was young; he never told us he went back there. You know that's where we're from. Did he tell you?"

Mrs. Williams just gave him a funny look and went on, "While he was there he got into some sort of trouble, a big fight, I think. Well, anyway, my brother shipped him back here to me after only about six months. And that was that. I didn't ask, and he didn't tell. But when he got back he was changed; something seemed to have scared him bad."

Just as Slick was leaning in, intent on hearing what was coming I got up off of the chair I was sitting on in her parlor and announced, "Well, I guess we've imposed on enough of your time. Thank you for what you've shared and we'll keep you informed on our progress with the memoir. Let's go Slick."

He gave me a strange look and said, "But Hap…"

"Let's go Slick," I said in a more forceful voice, still smiling at Mrs. Williams. I grabbed his arm and lifted him off of his chair and pulled him toward the door.

As we walked to the car, me dragging him by his arm, he stopped, turned toward me, pulling his arm out of my grip and stated, "I'm not going another step until you tell me what this is all about!"

I took a deep breath and paused long enough to let my anger at his insistence subside and responded, "Okay; here it is. We have the clues that we needed to help us solve what actually happened in Devon's room the night he was murdered!"

"MURDERED?" he shot back in disbelief.

"Yes, murdered. I believe he was murdered. But in order to be sure, you and I need to take a road trip."

Slick was now more confused than ever. All he could get out was, "To where?"

I smiled and said, "Buffalo!"

# 33

## The Buffalo Connection

**"You got some 'splainin' to do here Ricky!"**
**-Lucille Ball**
**From the "I Love Lucy Show"**

"You're going where!"

I knew Joanie wouldn't take this well. "Just for a few weeks; I think." Why did I have to add that.

"You think? What do you mean you think? **'You got some 'splainin' to do here Ricky!'"**

"Well, uh. You see Slick and I, when we went to talk to Mrs. Williams, we, uh…"

"Slick huh! I should have know he was involved in this somehow."

"We, uh, are planning to write a memoir about Devon's life and we, uh, well; we, uh, thought that it might, uh, be a good idea, uh, if we, well, you know…"

I could see the fire in her eyes as I stumbled along. I never could tell a good lie; that was Slick's department – and he wasn't here to bail me out of this one.

"Oh, I see. That makes perfect sense. Now, how about telling me the truth this time?"

"Okay, just give me a chance to explain what we learned from our visit with her. In fact, it would probably be good to get Slick and Susie over here to discuss it as a group. After all, he's involved too."

\*　　　　\*　　　　\*

"Nice going chump," Slick whispered to me as he walked past me to sit at the kitchen table next to Susie.

I didn't have time to explain to him what I did say, but he knew from what Joanie told Susie on the phone that I had blown it.

"Okay, who wants to go first?" Joanie said turning her glare from me to Slick and back again. Susie just sat there; she was loving it. She knew how Joanie could get when she was agitated; and she knew to let her alone when she was on a mission. Besides, I think that Susie always liked to see Slick and I squirm.

Slick jumped in before I could open my mouth. He knew it would be all over if I spoke; I would probably say something stupid, like the truth.

"Well you see, me and Hap were just sitting around with Devon's mom, you know, talking over old times when I had this idea to write something as sort of a memorial to Devon. Well, one thing led to another..."

"Why thank you Slick; enough of the BS! I'm not in the mood for this now. Hap; let's hear what you have to say. Maybe there'll be enough truth in your story to actually make some sense of why you two need to go to Buffalo. Well?"

I could see she was in no mood for anything BUT the truth. I glanced over at Slick who gave me a look that said, 'Okay; I tried. Now's the time that's reserved for the truth – that rare moment; so tell them.'

"It's like this..." I began, relating what we had found out about the cards and how that led us to look into his past with his sisters and brothers, and then with his mom. I told them how his mom told us about his stay in Buffalo.

"Now we need to find out what exactly happened there and how it relates to his murder – if there is any connection. That's all we have to go on," I said as the girls sat silent; amazed at what I had revealed.

"But what makes you think a little fight years ago has anything to do with his death? And what makes you so sure that it was murder when the coroner and the police seem to believe that it was death by overdose?" Susie questioned.

Slick jumped in with, "It's simple enough. Devon didn't have the money or the drug habit for us to believe that he would be doing something as hard as crack cocaine. That is, unless he was hiding a vast fortune and did these drugs when we weren't with him. Don't forget I used to live with him; and, if you remember, I moved in because he needed someone to help him pay his rent. Now that doesn't sound to me like he had much money; does it to you?"

I was quick to add, "You're right, he needed help paying his rent – but we also needed someone off of our living room couch!"

Slick snapped back in a sarcastic tone, "Well, I guess it worked out for everyone, didn't it?"

"Alright boys; we don't need a 'cat fight' – or should I say 'dog fight'?" Susie said in a mocking voice.

Joanie, with her characteristic concern for detail added, "So how long do you plan to stay there? And what do you hope to find? You know that if you're going there to find a killer, you're putting your own lives at risk. I don't think that if someone there did kill Devon he is going to say to you, 'Okay boys, you got me. I killed Devon and I'm ready to turn myself in.' There's going to be danger for the both of you; and quite frankly, as much as I'd like to see this thing resolved, it's not worth it to me to see you two dead."

Susie quickly added, "That's right. I wouldn't want anything to happen to you Hap…or you either Slick."

We all looked over at her at this remark. I could see that I wasn't the only one who found it strange for her to say that, especially since she and Slick were living together now. Slick looked over at me, and I could see a hurt expression on his face that he was trying to hide. He shook his head and put on a fake smile and said, "Well, I'm glad to see someone cares about me – even if it's just a little."

Susie caught her mistake and quickly said, "You know how I feel about you Slick. I was just worried about Hap, 'cause you know how he always manages to get himself caught up on the short end of the stick, so to speak. And I know how you've always been able to take care of yourself just fine."

We could see Susie's trademark phony smile; the one her mother taught her long ago. We all knew her well enough to know there was something devious buried in her remark; and we all knew her well enough to know that we needed to let it go – we'd find out what was behind it sooner or later.

# 34

## Shufflin' off to Buffalo

**"If I didn't know any better...well, I wouldn't know any better!"**
**-Slick**

"Hap, Hap, HAP! I swear you're hard of hearing."

"No I ignore a lot," I responded under my breath. If Joanie only knew all of what I did hear and said she would've beat the life out of me long ago.

"What was that? Don't think I didn't hear that, smart ass!"

I'm sure she had to be guessing. I could barely hear myself say it.

"Yes dear. What is it?"

"I swear you could sleep your life away. It's after seven and you told Slick that you'd pick him up at seven-thirty this morning to start your trip to Buffalo; remember?"

"Don't be so dramatic...at least not this early in the morning. You know I'm not a morning person. My stuff's already packed and in the car and I'll be ready in 15 minutes. That will give me 15 more to get to his apartment; plenty of time. Besides, you know Slick. He won't be ready for another half hour – at least."

"And please Hap; please remember what I told you. I want you to come back in one piece – alive! As soon as you find anything out let the police know and come home. Got it?"

"Of course; don't forget, I'm not a fool. I know when to run; and as soon as I have any proof that Devon's death wasn't self-inflicted I'll be on my way home – I promise."

"Be safe; I love you," Joanie said as we kissed goodbye. She doesn't say it often, but she let's me know all the time in so many other ways.

"I love you too. And we'll be back before you can miss us."

"But I'm missing you already," she added with a laugh.

"Yeh, right back at ya!" I said as I began to laugh along with her.

"And don't forget to leave the keys to the car under the driver's floor mat. Susie's dropping me off later today to pick it up at the bus terminal downtown. Park it where I can find it too.

\*       \*       \*

We needed to be at the Greyhound Station on Front St. by 8:00 a.m.; our bus was scheduled to leave at 8:15. Since Slick and Susie lived at the Carolina Apartments on Market and Fifth, I

could pick him up on the way. We figured we could borrow Sarge's old Studebaker when we got to Buffalo. He didn't drive much anymore. He just used it to go to his AA meetings, and then to the corner store to get his case of Genny Cream Ale. As long as we got the beer for him he didn't mind missing the meetings too much. Although he did once tell us that the reason he drank so much was because the meetings made him stressed and he needed the beer to calm back down. Somehow he made
sense.

"Hap, where've you been? I've been up, packed and ready to go for over an hour," Slick said before I could even sit down and drink the cup of coffee Susie had just put on the counter for me.

"Slick, it's just seven-thirty now. When have you ever been early for anything?" I couldn't believe my ears. "Just
messing with you," he said with a grin.

"Come on Hap, wake up and drink the coffee. When have you ever known Slick to be on time for anything?" Susie added.

"Alright you two; it's too early for me. Give me five minutes to sit quietly and wake up. Slick, I left the trunk open so you could put your stuff there. If you have anything you want to put in the cooler for the trip, it's on the back seat. Okay?" I said as I fell into a semi-conscious state – at least for a minute or two.

As Slick grabbed his things and headed out the door to my car Susie moved her chair close to mine, leaned in toward me, grabbing my arm and pressing her chest against it and said in not much louder than a whisper, "Now Hap I want you to be very careful there. Don't get in over your head. I want you to come back to me in one piece…I mean to us, Joanie and me, that is."

I turned toward her and gave her a strange look. She caught herself, and continued, "And make sure Slick doesn't do anything stupid either. You know how much I care about the both of you. You're more than my best friends."

Just as she was finishing Slick came lumbering back through the door that leads to the hall and down the back stairs to where my car was parked and announced, "Well, that's just fine!"

At that, I pulled myself out of Susie's clutches, jumped up and began to try to explain, stumbling over my words, as if I had been the one who had initiated this situation, "I wasn't doing anything…Susie and I were just…"

With a momentary confused look Slick remarked, "What in the hell are you babbling about? I'm talking about the flat tire on your car. Did you drive here with it so that I would feel sorry for you and change it. Well, you're very wrong. You can change it yourself!"

I was so relieved that he didn't think I was moving in on his girl that I shot back, "Sure. Not a problem. I'll go take care of it right away. You just sit down with Susie and say your goodbyes and I'll go change the tire lickity-split!"

I ran out the door, happy that that was all it was. I could hear Slick say to Susie, "What in the world has gotten into him? I've never seen him so happy to change a flat tire before?"

Susie responded loud enough so that I would hear it, "Who knows. Hap's always been a bit kooky. You know that." So

off we went; 'Shufflin' off to Buffalo!'

# Part V: dal segno al coda

While notes and chords depict the lines,
The melody remains.
And double bars with double dots –
Recycle once again.

D.S. al coda's where to go,
It shows the place to be.
No matter what the style or mode –
Life's rhythm is the key.

# 35

## Don't You Never Lie to Your Momma!

**"Mom, you're always so pleasant. I don't know how you do it."**
**-Hap**

"I don't see why you won't stay here with me at Sarge's. Your mom is just down the street and your brother Jeffrey is around the corner."

"Look Slick, I need to spend some time with my mom. I know she's doing fine now, and would probably prefer it if she didn't have to wait on me; but I feel like I would be insulting her if I didn't stay there…at least for a night. I know it's probably more for me than her, but I've got to do it. After that, you and I can stay at Jeffrey's. He's single and has an extra bedroom and a pull out sofa-bed in the living room; we're a bit too old to be staying with mom or dad for more than a night."

"Okay. I guess you're right. Sarge would probably begin to get on my nerves after more than 24 hours alone with him. Besides, we're not here for a visit; we came on a mission."

After a pause I could see those mice spinning the wheel in Slick's head; and before I could stop him he said, "Hey, we can have the best of both worlds if we play it right. Your mom's a great cook and Sarge has always got plenty of Genny Cream Ale in the 'frig; not to mention his many war stories. We can eat at your mom's, drink with Sarge and have a good laugh, and then head over to Jeffrey's for the night to sleep it off. How's that sound?"

"Slick, for once in your life you're beginning to make perfect sense to me!"

*       *       *

My mom had invited Jeffrey over to eat dinner with us, but he said he'd rather let me spend some alone time with her – and Slick. Besides, he told her, he would get to see me when we came over to sleep at his apartment. He'd have plenty of time with us. Somehow I get the feeling he's still not a big fan of Slick's. Oh, he doesn't dislike him; he just (as he used to say), 'Can only take Slick in small doses'.

Anyway, that suited me just fine. I knew Slick would be engrossed in whatever pasta dish mom made, and that would give me time to catch up on her life.

And I guess I did miss knocking back a few with Sarge and listening to him describe in detail how he won the war all by himself! And the drunker he got, the better the stories. I've often thought – if only he wrote them down; what a great piece of fiction that would be.

"Good evening Mrs. Pozner. You look lovely tonight – as usual. Here; I've brought some flowers to brighten up the dinner table – but I see you're doing that already."

Mom just looked at me and rolled her eyes. She knew how every time Slick was around her he all of a sudden became **'Eddie Haskell'** from the **"Leave it to Beaver"** show.

"Why thank you Slick; and I see you bought these this time. I'm so glad you thought to leave the price tag on so I could see what a bargain you got; and, of course I'm even happier to see my flower garden still in tact."

"You're more than welcome. I got them down at Tops. They were on sale; I guess 'cause they were getting pretty old. But I think they look okay."

"Of course they do. Why, I wouldn't have been able to tell how close to death they really are without you telling me. Thank you again. I'll just go get a vase and put them right here on the table so that we can enjoy their last few precious moments, while we eat our dinner," mom remarked. She had a way of smiling and paying you a compliment while insulting you – all at the same time. I swear she makes Southern women look like pikers, and she doesn't even have to say, 'bless your heart'.

After the usual delicious meal my mom prepared for us we sat and drank a few glasses of red wine – 'Dago Red' as my dad used to call it; Chianti to those 'non-Italians'.

"So Slick, what brings you two back home all of a sudden? I'm surprised you came without the girls. Although I can understand that they probably needed a break."

"Mom, you're always so pleasant. I don't know how you do it. I guess that's why I love you so much," I said with a sarcastic smile.

"Hap, you know I love you…and Slick, but you must admit that you both are a bit high maintenance."

"You do have a point there. Well, we came home because we had been thinking about…" Just as I was about to tell my best lie, she cut me off.

"Now Hap. I believe I was talking to Slick. I thought your dad and I taught you better than to interrupt."

I knew what she was doing. She knew that she was the only person that I was able to lie to with a straight face. I don't know why; I guess maybe because I loved her and wouldn't want her to know why we really came back. I didn't want her to worry.

Slick, on the other hand, could lie to anybody – and get away with it; that is, except for my mom.

She paused a moment to collect herself, smiled and said, "Now where was I; oh, yeh. Slick what brought the two of you back here? Not that I'm not overjoyed to see you both, but it seems odd that you'd come back home so suddenly."

"Well, ah, ah; well we…" Slick went on mumbling and stumbling until he finally gave it up.

"WHAT! No you are not. Hap, if your father were still alive he would be adamant about this; and Slick, even Sarge would tell you you're both crazy."

"Mom; this is something we have to do. Devon was our friend. If it were me or EVEN Slick you would want someone to find out who was responsible; now wouldn't you?"

Slick looked at me and just said, "Thanks a lot."

"Well, I suppose so. But can't you leave it to the authorities?" I could see the worry start to spread across her brow.

"Mom; do you remember one of dad's favorite quotes? I believe he said it was President Ford who said, **'A government big enough to give you everything you want is a government big enough to take from you everything you have.'** He was teaching self-reliance and so was dad. Besides, we tried talking to the police. They said there was no evidence of foul play and the case was closed as far as they were concerned."

"I don't know about this, but I do understand. It's hard for me to see you and your brother, and especially Slick, as anything else but little children – my children."

Slick just shook his head and grunted, "Thank you too."

Mom continued, "But I guess you've grown to be a man, and you've got a man's job to do – so be careful; please." I could see her eyes well up with tears as she said this.

I tried to cheer her up with, "Of course mom. You know me and Slick. When have we ever gotten into trouble?"

Slick never did understand the word 'rhetorical' and stated, "Well, the time the row boat sunk on lake Erie with us in it; you remember the big storm. Or, how about the snow tunnels we made, when you all thought that I was buried alive in one of them and got the police and fire departments here…"

"Alright Slick; BASTA!" as my dad used to say to Jeffrey and me when he wanted us to stop whatever it was that we were doing that was getting on his nerves.

"No thanks. I'm full," Slick shot back with a grin.

"No Slick; basta, basta, not pasta. That's Italian for 'enough," mom interjected.

"Mom; he knows what it means. He was just playing dumb…this time."

"Hey!" Slick said as he feigned being insulted.

# 36

## Drinkin' Buddies?

**"You don't call me Sir; I work for a living!"**
**-Sarge**

"Now Hap, I have to warn you. Sarge is in one of his rare moods tonight. I think, for some crazy reason, he's happy to see us."

"Slick, I think for some crazier reason, I'm kinda looking forward to seeing Sarge again, too. He's probably been a bit lonely since your mom died and you moved away. I know he does go down to my mom's house and have coffee with her just about every morning, but he really misses Lulu," I said as I found myself getting sentimental over, of all people, Sarge.

But I guess he isn't so bad. It's just that I can't seem to forget that first night I slept over Slick's as a kid and saw Sarge come home in a drunken rage and beat Slick so bad. I'll never get over that.

"Yeh, I suppose you're right; but when I left to come to your mom's for dinner he was already in rare form. Oh, and by the way, he just picked up another case of Genny Cream Ale for us. So be prepared for the long haul; if you get my drift."

"It's gonna be a long evening of drinking and war stories, right," I said with a sigh.

"You got it!" Slick responded.

*       *       *

"Hi boys; good to see you. I'm sure you had a good meal; Hap's mom is a great cook. Slick, I hope you used your best manners. I don't want anyone thinking that your mom and I raised a slob."

"I love you too, dad. Of course I did; what do you think I'd do – fart at the table?" Slick shot back at his dad as he responded.

"While this makes for great conversation I think we should change the subject. Oh, and by the way, he didn't fart or even burp; amazing!" I had to add.

"Alright, that's enough of pick on Slick night. How about that beer you promised us Sarge?" Slick changed the subject to one we all liked.

"Right there in the cooler, packed in ice," Sarge said with a smile.

"I see you've been doing some redecorating Sarge. What do you call it, early trailer trash?" Slick said in his most sarcastic tone.

"No smart ass. I put the big ice chest here in the living room so we wouldn't have to walk out to the laundry room to get our beer. I figured we'd be putting them away pretty fast. And the trash can is here to toss your empties in when you're done. How's that    for planning. You know back when I was training my
men…"

"Okay Sarge, BASTA!" Slick said.

"Jesus Christ all Friday! What in the hell are you talking about, pasta?" Sarge replied.

At this point, I needed to jump in between them, so to speak. "Listen; I'd like to drink to the two of you. Two of the most…ah…interesting people I know."

That stopped the two of them in their tracks. I knew it was about to erupt into a fight between Sarge and Slick, and I didn't want to be around to see who won. I knew I was in for a long night if this was how it was starting out. They were already at each others throats and they weren't even drunk yet!

We all sat there silent for a few minutes. Then, out of nowhere Sarge hit us with, "Why did you boys really come back to Buffalo?"

We were both stunned by his remark. I responded, "We're writing a memoir about our friend Devon you see…" Sarge
interrupted, "Don't try to bullshit a bullshit artist!
I'm only going to say it one more time. Why did you boys come back?"

Slick and I looked at each other, then at Sarge. We could see he was in no mood for any lies; mine or Slick's.

I spoke up first, "You see Sir…"

You don't call me Sir; I work for a living," Sarge shot at me.

Oh, how I missed those days. "Sorry Sarge. We're here to find out how Devon died. We think there's a Buffalo connection. Slick had the idea that maybe someone from Devon's past was the cause of his death."

I continued laying out our plan, such as it was, of how we hoped to find his killer.

"Hold it; hold it right there! When in the hell has Slick ever had an idea that didn't get you both into trouble?"

As soon as the words left his lips Sarge must have realized that he was talking about Slick in the third person. He turned to Slick and said, "Sorry son; no offense."

Slick looked a little hurt, but responded, "None taken." Sarge went on, just as in the old days, "My men know the potential dangers that a mission poses, and they take the necessary precautions to avoid them. Do you hear me?"

We both responded in unison, "Yes Sarge!"

"Now if you're going into a covert operation there are things you need to know; you need a good plan, code words you both understand, and above all, you have to know when it's time to get the hell out of there."

Sarge was making perfect sense. I began to think that his experience as a drill instructor could be a real asset to Slick and me.

For the next few hours he filled us with details of how we should handle this operation and how important it was to

~ 224 ~

have code words for things we needed to communicate with each other when anyone else was present, especially anyone involved in Devon's death.

As Sarge went on point by point, I marveled at how much he really did know. I could see that Slick was a bit surprised and amazed at his dad as well. In fact, I thought I could see, for the first time, a little pride showing in his smile as he listened intently to every word that Sarge uttered.

When he was done, Sarge paused and looked at the two of us and ended with, "Now boys, you know I love you; and I think this is not a good idea; but I do know that, just like 'The Big One', this is a war that needs to be fought. So do me proud, and watch each other's back. Got it? And after you talk with this Harry guy you come back and we'll lay out a plan and I'll get you men the necessary gear for your mission."

We both smiled at each other and said, "Absolutely, Sarge." It was like getting his blessing.

I thought that this would be a good time to put the conversation on a lighter note; so I turned to Sarge and said the magic words.

"Sarge; you got any good war stories for us tonight? How about the time you trained the men that lead the ground forces in Operation Torch back in November of '42."

As the trademark Graham shit-eating grin crossed his face Sarge responded with, "Oh, so you know about that battle." Not that we haven't heard it since we were about six years old – over and over and over...

~ 225 ~

Then he began to tell his tale, "Well, let me tell you. While I was stateside my men were there doing me proud. Yeh, they were in the thick of it over in North Africa that year. It was in November of 19-and-42. Why I heard that one of my best recruits even…"

Slick leaned over to me as Sarge was just getting started and said, "Hap are you nuts? We've heard this one a thousand times before; and do you remember how long it takes? Every time he tells it he somehow manages to make it longer. Last time it was over three hours long."

"I know, but at least it's better than seeing you two rolling around on the living room floor trying to knock each others teeth out," I added.

"I'd definitely win that one; he has false teeth you know; and I'm surprised you didn't ask him how he lost them. Then we could have heard how he lost them one at a time in boxing matches on his way to losing the Golden Gloves title back in '35. Besides, I'm sure I could take him now; my head's harder than his."

All I could say was, "Sometimes it's hard to tell," as Sarge rambled on, never noticing that we weren't paying a bit of attention; every once in a while giving us a big grin.

It was pushing two in the morning when he ran out of beer and stories (thank God). Sarge was pretty much talked out by then; he had replayed all the battles from the North African Operation Torch to the Guadalcanal Campaign and on to the

Normandy Invasion (including D-Day). It made me tired just listening to it.

"...and that my boys was what real men were made of; not the sissy boys we have today," Sarge said as a final note to his otherwise brilliant account of every battle – hill and beach, taken from 1942 to 1945.

By the time Sarge had finished his stories the three of us were pretty tired and drunk.

Slick turned to his dad and, in a serious tone, said, "Hey Sarge, why didn't you ever date after mom died? You were quite the lady's man when she was alive as I remember."

"Son, it took a lot of years, but I finally realized how much your mom meant to me. And I wasn't about to get married again. Who knows you might get up with some woman that wouldn't let you drink, smoke or pass out every night. Ha!"

He could see that Slick was being serious so he continued, "I did date a few times about four or five years after your mom passed, but I had a problem...you know."

Slick began to laugh, "You mean you couldn't get it on with them?"

Sarge shot him a stern look and replied, "You might say that. So I went to my stupid-ass doctor; I call him that because in all of the years I've gone to him he hasn't helped me once."

That remark begged the question, so I asked, "Then why do you go to him? Why not go to another doctor?"

"Hap, do you know how hard it is to find a doctor you can get drunk with now-a-days?" "He's

your drinking buddy?"

Slick interrupted, "So Sarge, what did he tell you?"

As serious as can be Sarge gave us the diagnosis, "Well he said, of all things, that I had some new disease; I think that you get it from animals! Now I've read about 'Leopard-se', you know – in the Bible and all; I heard about it years ago in the readings at mass, when I used to go to church – but this is something new."

"What in the hell are you talking about?" Slick said, losing his patience with Sarge.

"He said I had 'a reptile dysfunction', whatever the hell that is. Anyway, it seems that's what's causing my lack of…well, you know. I reminded him that I had the Shingles a few years back and that made me look like a reptile, so maybe they're connected."

Slick looked at him with a puzzled expression and asked, "What did he say to that?"

"Well, I guess I kinda impressed him with my medical prowess; he said that I should be the doctor 'cause I obviously know a great deal more than he does about medicine. What do you think about that boys? Old Sarge, M.D."

I couldn't help myself; I started laughing hysterically. I was laughing so hard I began to choke.

In response to my seeming emergency Slick jumped up and ran over to me screaming to Sarge, "Grab him and stand him up. I'll give him some Hind-lick Remover! Susie showed me how to do this."

At that point I fell off of the ottoman I was sitting on and began to laugh even harder, rolling on the floor holding my sides; partly to keep them off of me, and partly because they hurt from laughing so hard.

Finally, I caught my breath and sat up, still on the floor, and said, "You have no idea how much I missed being with you two."

At that, Sarge stood up, belched, scratched his ass and then his head and said, "I'm going to bed. You boys can stay up and finish the beer."

Slick just mumbled, "What beer?"

As he headed toward the bathroom he turned around toward Slick and me and said, "I guess I'm getting old."

"Why's that Sarge?" I asked.

"'...cause I can walk to the bathroom without falling down."

He paused, as if to collect his thoughts and said, "Good night boys. I'm glad you came. Be safe, and don't forget what I told you, okay?"

We both just laughed and said good night. I think it was more of the fact that he had been talking so much he couldn't drink fast enough to get as drunk as he used to.

"Slick. What do you say we get out of here and head over to Jeffrey's. He's probably asleep by now, but I have his spare key to get us in."

Slick responded, "We might as well, all the beer is gone."

~ 229 ~

Then he turned to me with one of his more serious looks. I knew he was going to bring up our mission here; and the advice Sarge had given us.

"I hate to admit it, but Sarge is right. This probably isn't one of my better ideas."

I could see that even Slick was worried. In a strange way I found that comforting.

# 37

## Jeffrey to the Rescue?

"Fredo, you're my older brother, and I love you. But don't ever take sides with
anyone against the Family again. Ever."
-Michael Corleone
from "The Godfather: Part II"
by Mario Puzo


"Hap, Hap, HAP! Are you listening to me?"

"How can I not? You're shouting at me from two feet
away!"

Jeffrey had a way of making himself heard, even as a kid.
It was barely daybreak, Slick and I had just gotten in to his flat a few
hours before, and here he was waking us. I had just gotten
comfortable amidst the strewn clothes and things lying all over the
bed where I was trying to sleep.

He was always the slob of the family and his upper flat on
Spaulding Street, just a few blocks from mom's house, was just
how I remembered it. He had clothes on the floor, dishes and
boxes with left over food on every end table and counter

space you could find. There were cobwebs on the windows and some green stuff around the edges of his bath tub. I knew that mom had not been there lately. She would have cleaned the place up for him and then scolded him for not taking better care of his place. Of course, he would beg forgiveness and continue to be a slob, knowing mom would come over every once in a while to clean it again. And so the cycle would continue.

I understood the mess on the floor and counters, but how he got food on the ceiling of the kitchen was beyond me. But I didn't ask; I just didn't walk under it.

And I wouldn't have minded staying in that pig sty if it weren't for his habit of butting in on everything. He always put his two cents in, even when it wasn't wanted; but, I must admit, this time he had a point. Just like Sarge told us a few hours before – we needed a plan. Jeffrey pointed out that we also needed bait – and we needed him.

He had been nagging me to let him be a part of our mission. I was too tired to argue with him; he had caught me at a weak moment – he always seemed to be able to do that.

"Okay; you're in. But please don't tell mom that I let you talk me into this. You know how she can get," I extolled Jeffrey.

He stopped and with a pitiful look said, "Look it Hap; I think Slick is right. He told me to tell mom the truth about my helping you. I can't lie to her."

Knowing how good Jeffrey could lie, I knew he had to be messing with me; so I looked at him with a straight face, grabbed him by the arms and said, **"Fredo, you're my older brother, and I love you. But don't ever take sides with anyone against the Family again. Ever."**

At that we all burst out laughing. Ever since we saw **Godfather II,** Jeffrey and I have been quoting lines back and forth.

After a few minutes he said, "Alright, you got me. She'll never know. We'll be done with this whole thing before she even gets an inkling as what's going on," Jeffrey said with his devilish smile.

"Jeffrey, you're beginning to scare me. You're sounding more and more like Slick every day."

"Hey; is that a nice way to talk about me. I am right here you know," Slick added, somewhat insulted by my, well, insult.

"Sorry. Now I think our first move it to talk to Devon's uncle, Harry Chambers down on Peach St. Mrs. Williams gave me his address and phone number. Let's give him a call and see if he can help us; but remember, as far as he knows we're writing a memoir on Devon. This is not an attempt to find his killer; got it?" I knew Slick knew how important this ruse was, but I was worried about Jeffrey. He might slip.

"Don't worry Hap. We got it!" Jeffrey said with an air of confidence. Jeffrey to the rescue – what a thought!

But before we go there's one stop I need to make this morning. There's someone I must see first. Slick, I think it would do you good to meet him. Jeffrey, we'll pick you up on the way to the east side. We shouldn't be more than an hour or so."

"Sure. Tell him I said hello, and I'll see him Sunday," Jeffrey said as Slick and I got into Sarge's old Studebaker.

"Where're we going?" Slick questioned.

"Just drive," I said with a smile as we pulled out of the driveway and onto Spaulding. "We're headed to St. Stephen's to see Fr. Christopher.

# 38

## A Final Blessing

"Well, according to Sarge, that's my dad, you guys look like the grim reaper."
-Slick

"Hap, what are we doing here at St. Stephen's? This is no time to relive your Catholic high school education. We've got more important things to do right now."

"Slick, if you would just stop rambling for a minute I'll explain. I need, no we need, to see Fr. Christopher. He helped me out a lot when I went here. You remember the trial and all of that stuff that almost got me kicked out; well, Fr. Christopher saved my ass on that one. He also has a connection with my mother and father. We need to see him to, well, to get his blessing. Besides, he knows the east side of Buffalo as good as anyone, and I'll bet he probably knows people there who can help us if we need. Relax, you'll like him. He's pretty cool; and wait 'till you hear some of his expressions; there every bit as good as your family's."

"Okay, but I get nervous around priests and nuns – you know that. Ever since we went to Catechism when we were in grade school I haven't been comfortable around them."

"Well, maybe if you didn't get into so much trouble they might have not smacked you around so much."

"You may have a point there, Hap."

*     *     *

"Fr. Christopher!" I grabbed his hand to shake it, and then gave him a hug.

"Hap, your mother called me yesterday and told me you were in town. How nice of you to take the time to visit this old monk."

"I couldn't come home without seeing you. Fr. Christopher I want you to meet my best friend, Slick."

As they shook hands Slick said, "It's nice to meet you Father, Hap has told me about how much you helped him when he went to school here. I got to tell you I was expecting you to look different."

I could see disaster looming just around the corner, but it was too late to stop him.

"Well laddie, what might it be that I was supposed to look like?" Fr. Christopher asked, turning on his Irish brogue.

"Well, according to Sarge, that's my dad, you guys all look like the grim reaper. You know, that guy with the hood and the sickle and skeleton hands. I'll have to tell him that you look like normal people."

Fr. Christopher turned to me and gave me a look that said, 'is he for real?' I just shrugged my shoulders.

Fr. Christopher turned back to Slick and responded with, "Hap told me all about you. In fact, when he attended St. Stephen's I used to think he was making you and your family up; We were all a little worried about him. It was hard to believe you and your family were real; but here you are as real as can be. Will miracles never cease. It's just a shame that you didn't attend St. Stephen's; you and Fr. Aloysius would have many a story to tell today; that's certain!"

Before either of us could shut Slick up he added, "Hap, you remember what you told me when you first came to St. Stephen's? You told me that they had some letters after their names."

Fr. Christopher interjected, "Yes we do. They're O.F.M."

Slick responded with, "That's right. Remember you told me that they stood for 'Old Fat Monks'. Ha!"

I could feel my face turning red as Fr. Christopher gave me a stern look; but it quickly turned into a smile.

Slick went on, "Did you guys ever change that?"

Fr. Christopher could see what I've been dealing with these many years and realized it was hopeless to be logical with him. He responded, "Well, no Slick. Unfortunately those initials were monogrammed on all our towels, bathrobes and handkerchiefs. We decided to just change what the letters stood for to 'Order of Friars Minor'."

Slick thought about it for a few seconds, put on a big smile and said, "Good thinking!"

With that Slick turned to me and said, "He is pretty cool Hap."

Besides the letters, what else Slick didn't know was that Fr. Aloysius, referred to as 'the Destroyer' by all of the students and half of the faculty, was the Prefect of Discipline; the one who you are sent to when you get into trouble in class, or anywhere else on the school grounds for that matter. Fr. Christopher was right, Slick and 'the Destroyer' would have seen a lot of each other!

"What brings you two to town? I hope you're not in any trouble; are you?" He folded his hands behind his back and tilted his head down, looking over his glasses at us in that 'fatherly' way he had.

"Well, Father we're here on a mission of sorts. We came here to find our friend's killer; and I wanted you to give us your blessing and prayers – 'cause we're gonna need them."

"Let's sit down in the study where you can tell me all about it."

So we did. I told him about Devon and what we hoped to find out. He said he would be there for us to get our backs if we needed. Through friends he had in that neighborhood and other clergy on the east side that he knew he would do what he could to help us find our answers and to stay safe.

"Hap, I'm glad you didn't try to feed me any malarkey because when your mother and I talked yesterday she told me all about your plans here. I've already made some phone calls around town, so know that there will always be an angel watching out for you. May God bless you, in the name of…"

After we said our goodbyes he walked us out to the parking lot and saw Sarge's old Studebaker.

"What a fine machine you men have here; just what you'll need to be successful in your quest. I had one of these before the war. It was a great car. Now you boys be safe and remember I'll be there to watch out for you – in some way or another."

# 39

## The Best Laid Plans...

**"Hey, my dad was a D.I. during the war too. Maybe you knew him; his
name is Sarge!"**
**-Slick**

"Mr. Chambers; it's nice to meet you. And thanks for being willing to help us with our writing project. You know Devon meant a lot to us, Slick and me. This is my brother Jeffrey; he didn't really know Devon that well, but he wanted to help us out with getting information for the memoir."

A big smile crossed his face as he said, "Please sit down, and call me Harry – my daddy was Mr. Chambers," he said as he began to laugh.

He seemed like a happy kind of man, content with his life. I could see by the lines on his face that he had weathered a great deal in his life. He stood tall and strong for a man in his 60s; his hands were big and powerful, and rough – rough from many years of laying track and driving spikes on the Erie Lackawanna Railroad, where he had worked for nearly 40 years. The only thing that interrupted his work there was the war – World War II; when we got into it he signed up for the infantry and headed for North Carolina.

From what Devon's mom had told us he had sent her money each month to help support her and her six children, she being a widow and all. Devon's dad was killed when the children were young and his wife was barely 30 years old.

"Your sister, Mrs. Williams, told us a little about you and your situation here. I could tell from the way she beamed as she talked about you that she really loved and admired her older brother. I guess you two are still pretty close, even though you're many miles apart," I said as sort of a lead in for him.

"That's right son. Georgia and me have been tight since we was kids. Maybe 'cause I was the oldest of the bunch of us and she was my baby sister; maybe that's what made us close. From the time she was a baby she would look up at me and grin from ear to ear. I'd just laugh and hold her in my arms. It's been that way ever since. So I guess you could say distance makes no difference; she's always been my favorite."

The three of us all smiled as he went on relating his story about Devon and his family.

"Big Charlie, that's what we used to call Devon's dad, he was a good church-going man. To see him you'd think that he was a killer or something; but he was kind and gentle as could be, and he had a heart as big as the ocean. It was when Devon, the baby of the family, was only two years old that these two men

~ 241 ~

stopped Charlie as he was walking with Devon down Pine Street. They exchanged words; I suspect they mistook him for some other guy who owed them money for drugs. The neighborhood was getting kind of rough at that time. These rough looking white guys had moved into the area and began selling drugs to us colored folk. Some of them were from that same biker club that I believe got Devon."

We could see his demeanor change as he was brought into the present and the weight of Devon's death was on him. He seemed to blame himself for it.

As he sort of chuckled between what looked like tears he said, "You know, us colored folk all look alike to you white guys, right?"

We didn't know what to say as he paused and stared at us. The three of us began to squirm a bit; and then he laughed and went on.

"They took him for someone else and stabbed him to death right there in broad daylight, and right in front of his baby boy, Devon – a sight no one, least a two year old child, would ever forget."

He paused for a moment, took a deep breath, and then said, "It was shortly after the funeral I told my sister, Georgia, that I was sending her and her family to live down south – in a little town called Wilmington in North Carolina. There she could start over and raise her six children in a quiet, safe place. I knew of this place 'cause of my late wife Josie. She was born and raised there."

We were all mesmerized by what he had told us. I could see Slick just waiting for a chance to jump in; he had a million questions I was sure. He always has a million questions.

"Harry," Slick interrupted as Harry stopped, thinking he had told us all we needed to know, "how did you meet your wife if you lived in Buffalo and she lived in Wilmington?"

He just laughed his big bellowing laugh at Slick's question.

"You are a curious bunch, now aren't you? I s'pose I should feel privileged that you want to listen to my stories. Most young folk today don't care about what we old folk have to say. So I'll tell you," he grinned as he spoke, showing a handful of teeth left in his strong, square jaw.

"In 19-and-41, when our country was attacked by those Jap-bastards at Pearl Harbor, I did like every able-bodied man did then – I enlisted in the Army to fight for my country. I was just over thirty years old at the time; older than many of the young men who were enlisting. I guess my age, my color and my working on the railroad as a foreman at that time made the Army think that I would be a good D.I. So they first sent me down to Camp Davis in Holly Ridge, NC for my basic training and began my stint as a drill instructor; and then later on, near the end of the war, to Fort Dix where I completed my time. But it was when I was stationed at Camp Davis that I met my wife, Josie. She was a sight; young, beautiful and full of fire. She worked on base in the mess hall. I'm not sure if it was her long, shapely legs or her fried chicken legs that got me first…," he said with a laugh.

"...but we hit it off right away, and, when my orders came in that I was being sent to Fort Dix, I told her 'I shall return' – like General MacArthur said when he first left the Philippines. And I did. We married four months later and I brought her here to this very house we sit in now, where we lived for seven years together until her death on February 29 in 19- and-52."

When he said that a chill ran down my spine; that was the day I was born! Slick and Jeffrey both knew that and they shot me a glance acknowledging it. I gave them a stern look, as if to say, 'Don't either of you dare tell this poor man. It's something that wouldn't help him.'

Before either of them could speak I said, "I hope this didn't bring up things you'd rather not talk about."

"Thanks Hap, but I think I needed to tell someone. After all these years if felt good to have a good audience. I know we hardly know each other, but I felt like I could tell you." He paused to compose himself, and then with a big laugh said, "Besides I don't often get to talk about my favorite subject – ME!"

At that, we all began to laugh.

"Now boys, I want to hear about you all."

We told Harry about ourselves, our families, and our friendship with Devon. It was then that the tone of the conversation changed abruptly.

"Now that the formalities are out of the way we can cut the bullshit." His smile turned to a stern glare as he looked from Slick to me, and then to Jeffrey. It made us all freeze; speechless, motionless in our chairs.

Finally, I got the nerve to say something, "I'm sorry; I don't understand."

No sooner than the words left my lips than he broke in with, "Don't be alarmed; I know that you all loved Devon like a brother – and I'm not talking skin color." With this he laughed at his own pun. We were all too scared to even move.

"I loved him too, and I think I know why you're really here. Tell me if I'm wrong. You all think that you're going to play detective and find his killer, right?"

We were all stunned by this statement. Slick spoke up first, "How did you know; I mean, what gave us away?"

"Look boys; and I call you boys only because, compared to me you're all still wet behind the ears. I was here when Devon got into that trouble. I told his mother, my sister, that it was nothing and that it would be best if he came home. But that's not the whole truth of the matter. He did get into some trouble – with a biker gang called 'The King of Clubs'."

When he said that, Slick and I turned to each other and said, "The King of Clubs!"

Harry stopped his story and said, "What? What about 'The King of Clubs'?"

We told him about the cards on the bed and how the king of clubs was the only card that was face up. We didn't know at the time what it meant, but now we know that it was a clue that either Devon or his killer left for us.

Harry went on to tell us more about Devon's encounter with this gang. We all sat there in disbelief as Harry related the details that led up to Devon's fight with a guy called 'Jake the Snake' and how Jake had vowed to get him no matter how long it took.

"You see Devon was sent here because he was getting too wild for his mom to handle back in Wilmington. She thought that he might straighten out if he spent some time with me. You see I was a drill sergeant during the war and was pretty good at getting results..."

Slick's face lit up and he interrupted with, "Hey, my dad was a D.I. during the war too. Maybe you know him; his name is Sarge!"

At that we began to laugh hysterically; all except Slick, that is.

"Son; we were all called Sarge back then." Harry didn't know Slick and, while that comment struck him as odd, it was typical Slick to Jeffrey and me.

"As I was saying, she sent Devon here in hopes to keep him out of trouble, but instead he got into more than he could handle. I saw what Georgia meant about Devon from the moment he arrived. He rode in to Buffalo in late April on his old Indian motorcycle like he had something to prove. I have to tell you, it took me a few months for me to knock that big chip off he had sitting right on top of his shoulder. I think that, and what happened later, helped him, as I like to say, 'to find religion'."

He paused for a moment, looked at us as if he were trying to read our minds, and continued, "He met this guy they call Jake the Snake; from a biker club here on the east side. I have to say that this biker club didn't discriminate – they had members from all races and ethnic backgrounds. The only requirements for membership were you had to be from the East Side of town and you had to be BAD. After a short time, this Jake character befriended Devon and he began to hang out with him and his friends at a biker bar just down the street from where we sit."

We could see the lines in his forehead that showed him reliving that awful past. It was at this point his tone changed from one of a strong, determined man to that of someone who found life out of control. He was helpless to do anything to help Devon now.

"I don't know exactly what happened; but one night, about five and a half months after Devon came to live with me, he came home and, looking as scared as could be, announced that he needed to go back home right away. It was late fall and the weather was beginning to change; and you know what the weather in Buffalo is like, don't you."

He kind of chuckled at his remark. We all knew what he meant.

He began again, "He begged me to give him enough money to make the trip home. He was leaving that very night. In fact, he took only long enough to pack a few things, tie them on to his motorcycle and off he went into the night. I was especially

~ 247 ~

worried for him since it was mid November and, even though the weather had been unusually mild for that time of year in Buffalo, I knew how quickly that could change and bring down several feet of snow on my poor, scared nephew; anywhere from Erie, Pennsylvania to Richmond, Virginia. But he made it back to Wilmington okay."

He paused and looked at us for a moment; then hung his head and continued, staring at his fingers as they locked together in front of him.

"His mother called me shortly after he arrived at her house to thank me for looking out for him. She wanted to know why he came back so suddenly. I just told her that he had a little trouble and felt he needed to go home. I also told her, as Devon had asked, that he wanted to surprise her; that's why we didn't let anyone know that he was on his way home. I blame myself. I should have sent him back long before this trouble started." As he spoke these words we could see his eyes fill with tears.

"And that was the last I saw of him; but not the last I saw of Jake or his biker buddies. You see, Jake knew that Devon was staying with me here, but he didn't know where he was from or where he disappeared to. It wasn't more than a week before I started seeing, first one, then several bikes riding down my street and slowing as they passed, just staring at me as they rode by while I sat on my old rocker on the front porch. Once they got a few houses down they would rev their bikes and speed off."

"Didn't that worry you? Did you call the police?" Slick interrupted.

"Son, do you really think the police could, or would for that matter, do anything. These boys were just riding by. They weren't threatening me. They were just riding by, that's all."

"Did it end?" Jeffrey asked.

"Oh yeh, it did. I'd see them ride by less and less frequently; and, over the course of the next few months, it stopped altogether. As the years rolled by I forgot all about them. I thought that life had resumed its normal course and that chapter had ended. That is, until about a month and a half ago. It was then that I saw Jake coming down Peach Street and do his slow ride past my house. But this time when he passed he smiled and kind of waved his arm at me; like he was tipping his hat or saluting. He then started laughing and sped away. That was just after Devon died. And that was the last time I saw him or any of his buddies. And that was the last time any of us will ever see Devon."

At this he hung his head in his hands and began to sob. We all just sat their in silence. After a few minutes he wiped his eyes with his big, strong hands and sat up facing us once again.

He said, "I know who killed my nephew; I just can't prove it. That's how I know why you're here. It's more of a hope than an intuition. Please tell me I'm right and I'll help you find his killer and bring him to justice."

This put us in a state of shock; long enough for me to evaluate the options. We DID need him.

"Yes; you're right. And we do need you to help us. We're all from here, but we grew up on the south side of Buffalo, not the east side. We don't know the streets, or the people – or the gangs for that matter. You can help us out a lot."

"Not only me, but I've got a whole arsenal of friends, family, and neighbors for that matter, who would like to clean up this part of town – beginning with 'The King of Clubs'."

I turned to Slick and said, "The first thing we have to do is get a couple of bikes and some biker clothes in order to play the part – if we're going to infiltrate a biker gang."

"We're gonna do what!" Slick said caught by surprise.

"We need to get in to find out what happened to Devon," I responded.

After a moment Slick said, "You're right. And I know just the person who can help us out with what we need – Sarge!"

# 40

## Saddle Up & Head 'em Out...Yee Haa!

**"I don't want you men getting the idea that killing a man is fun; or even easy."**
**-Sarge**

"...and we need bikes." As Slick and I went down the list for Sarge we could see the wheels spinning.

"Sarge, don't you want to write this stuff down?" I asked.

"Soldier, when on the battlefield you don't have time to make a list. It's all up here. My mind is like a steel trap. When something goes in – it stays there. And that's something the two of you had better get used to being able to do; especially with the operation you're about to undertake."

Sarge was right; anything written might be seen by one of the bikers and that could cost us our lives. We had better be able to remember everything.

\*      \*      \*

While Slick and I had ridden motorcycles in the past we knew we needed some practice before riding up to real bikers. Sarge said he would help us get a couple of old Harleys to ride, and help us get 'back in the saddle' before we rode into any danger with that biker gang. We had to look like we had been riding all our lives. He also helped us out with how we needed to come across to 'the King of Clubs' members, if, and when we were able to infiltrate.

"Sarge, it's been almost a week and a half. Hap and I have trained with you for nearly 10 hours a day. We've sat on those old broken-down Harleys at least six of them each day. We're getting kind of anxious to start our 'mission', if you know what I mean."

"The military is not a democracy. We don't vote on things. You get orders from your superiors, and you follow them; is that clear!"

Sarge was in our faces as he spouted out military protocol to us. I was so caught up in the intensity of it that I snapped to attention and shot back, "Yes Sarge!"

Slick turned to me, gave me a funny look and just shook his head and said, "I got it Sarge."

"At ease; now then you'll need some equipment and a uniform – of sorts. I've got some stuff I picked up at the military surplus store and the Goodwill. I also got a hold of some stuff you'll need that you can't get in any store that will come in handy when you booby trap your place. Men, you also need a safe house

— a place that you live in on the east side. It can't be anything too nice; the dumpier, the better. You got to have some booby traps around the perimeter to keep you relatively safe when you sleep, or stop anyone from getting in to surprise you when you come back from being out. You'll need some pepper spray in case your cover gets blown and you need a way to make a quick exit…"

"Sarge, Sarge, SARGE! Sorry to interrupt you, but what's this about pepper spray? If we need a weapon, why not a gun or a knife?" Slick asked.

"No. That would be fool-hearty. If you have a gun you might get too cocky and get into a shoot out. I don't want you men getting the idea that killing a man is fun, or even easy. In the real world killing a man is not like you see on TV. And, as for a knife; haven't I told you both a million times, 'You don't bring a knife to a gun fight'. Those boys will have guns."

"Okay, so what good will pepper spray do us?" I asked, jumping into the conversation.

"It's the most weapon you'll need. If they pull a gun or knife, or if they outnumber you, you can spray them and make a quick getaway."

"Well what if they're not close enough for us to be able to spray them?" Slick questioned.

"Son, if you're not close enough, you'd better hope that they aren't close enough to hit you with a bullet. They won't be carrying rifles; they'll have handguns, and probably not very good ones. Handguns, despite what you've seen in the movies are only accurate for short distances; and that's if you're a good shot.

These guys would probably have to be with in a few feet to even hit you."

"That's fine, but what if they are close enough to hit us, but we're too far for the pepper spray to reach them? What do we do then?" I wondered out loud.

Sarge paused a moment, looked me straight in the eyes and said only one word in response, "Pray."

"Now who wants some grub?" Sarge said, changing his expression and the tone of the conversation.

"Now you're talking!" Slick shot back. And the two of them turned and walked into the house.

*    *    *

It was time. We had our place to stay on the east side; we had our bikes, biker clothes and gear – and a blessing from Fr. Christopher; not to mention one from old Sarge, as well. All that was left was to go and do it.

"Hap, you feeling okay?" Slick said as we sat at the curb on our bikes, just about ready to leave.

"I don't know Slick. You and I have done some pretty stupid things in the past. But I'm feeling like this is going to be worse than anything we've gotten ourselves into so far. I just hope we get out alive!"

# 41

## Jake the Snake & the King of Clubs

**"As my daddy always said, 'There are some people you just can't be nice to.'"**
**-Hap**

"Hap, do you really think that anyone is going to buy our act as bikers?" Slick said as he rode on the broken down Harley under him.

"Just concentrate on getting back in the saddle. Remember, it's been a few years since you and I rode bikes – and they weren't this big."

"...or this old. It would be nice if we had bikes that parts weren't falling off of," he added.

I responded with, "I remember how you plowed your new bike into the back of a car full of guys who were stopped talking to some girls walking down the sidewalk on Seneca Street. I guess you like bikes with parts missing!"

"Yeh well that doesn't help us now. We're still rolling into the thick of it with these half-dead machines," he said bringing us back into the present.

I admonished, reminding him with, "This was the best Sarge could do for us. Be thankful we didn't have to buy them ourselves or we'd be riding Schwinns!"

"I know, but still…"

I interrupted him, "But still nothing. This will at least get us into the club and maybe we'll be able to get to know this Jake character enough to find out if he had anything to do with Devon's death. Remember – this is about Devon, not our riding comfort!"

That snapped Slick back into reality, "I guess you're right – for once."

Jeffrey turned to Harry and said, "You see what I have to put up with? I swear they act more like brothers than Hap and I do."

Finally, Harry interrupted us with, "Now boys, Jeffrey and I are here as your back up. I've got people watching. This is my neighborhood, don't forget. The club is just down at the end of the block, and I found an upper flat for you that is vacant just three houses down from here. If you need us we'll be there in an instant. Find out what you can and get out; you hear me?"

Harry knew the danger and in the short time we knew each other he began to think of us as family. I do believe, despite his age, he and men of his generation have more guts and determination than any generation since; after all they are the greatest generation – the ones who fought in 'the war to end all wars'; World War II. And they won it!

As Slick and I mounted our bikes we could hear Jeffrey say, "Gentlemen, start your engines."

And off we went; scared, worried and excited about what might happen.

*    *    *

It took almost two and a half weeks of Slick and me hanging out at 'The King of Clubs' bar before Jake even acted like he saw us; but we knew he and his boys had been watching us all along – to see what we were up to. To them we were just a couple of out of town bikers who were pretty good at shooting eight ball. It was a Friday night when things finally began to happen for us in our quest to get inside this gang. It didn't take more than a few times up at the pool table that night before Jake began to show his curiosity as to who we were. Slick and I both were pretty good at eight ball, drunk or sober. And these poor slobs couldn't hit a ball in if it was hanging on the lip of the pocket.

"You boys shoot a good game of pool. I've seen you come in quite a few times over the last two weeks or so. You come in, kick some ass on the pool table and walk out with your pockets lined with cash. Those boys you've been cleaning out are my boys."

~ 257 ~

I didn't know if he was pissed or not so I tried to play it very coolly and said, "Sorry man; if I knew they were your boys we would have given them a chance before we kicked their ass!"

At first he just looked at us and our hearts sank. I knew that they were going to kill us. But instead, a smile slowly washed across his face and he said, "No point wasting your time and talent; they're a bunch of losers. Ha!"

He started laughing and his 'boys' joined in. Slick and I let out a nervous laugh, trying not to show our angst.

Jake asked, "Where're ya boys from?"

"We're new in town; just stopped in town for a while on our way south. We just spent a year up in Toronto; stayed with some friends there. When we were looking for a place to crash here we saw your bikes outside and thought that we'd check this place out. Your boys have been pretty accommodating, losing their money and all, so we thought we'd hang out here while we're in town."

I could see that Jake wanted to know more about where we were from so I continued, "We're from the mountains of North Carolina, a place called Maggie Valley; just outside of Ashville," I said trying to feign a slight southern accent.

I didn't want him to know that we lived in Wilmington because he might make the connection, and I didn't want him to know we were from South Buffalo because of the rivalry between the different parts of the city.

"Is that a fact? Well then maybe we know some of the same people." He began to rattle off a handful of names, none of which were familiar to us. But when he began to name places and roads we were able to identify them and talk about them.

"Well, isn't that a coincidence. Me and my boys just got back from a place right in your neck of the woods; a place called Fontana Lake. Every fall they have a bike week there, so we thought we'd ride down to see what was going on. Besides, we wanted to ride that road down there that every biker needs to ride. And you being bikers and all; you must've ridden it a hundred times; right?" He was just testing us to see if we were really from that area.

"You're talking about the 'Tail of the Dragon'. That 11-mile stretch of road that winds through Tennessee and North Carolina, right. Oh yeh, we tamed it a few times!" Slick said with an air of confidence.

He just grinned; I guess he was satisfied with our details of the area.

Just then the bartender interrupted us. He was holding three beers – one for Slick, Jake and me. As he handed us the beer he pointed toward the bar at an old man just about falling off of his bar stool and said, "That old geezer over there sent these over to you. He said he was impressed with your shooting at the table."

Just as he was saying this the old guy turned toward us and doffed his old, dirty fedora – IT WAS FR. CHRISTOPHER!

He smiled at us and turned back around toward the bar without saying a word, paid his tab, got up and staggered out the door. Slick and I were stunned; but happy –he did have our backs.

After he left, Jake, who had gone to talk to the bartender, came back to the other side of the pool table where we were still standing and said, "Some of my boys tell me, besides taking their money at the pool table, you've been keeping them in beer. I guess we ought to show you some northern hospitality, right boys?"

When he said this, a few of his biker friends came over, surrounding us and began to laugh and said, "Right Jake."

I thought that we were in for it then; but as it turned out Jake wasn't kidding. He got the bar owner to put together a little party for us on Saturday – a southern pig-pickin' of all things.

\*       \*       \*

It seemed like an eternity mixing with those guys. Slick and I both felt it. We had roles to play that could cost us our lives. It wasn't until then that we realized that we were in over our heads; but it was too late to turn back now. We had to see this thing through. We had to keep reminding ourselves that it was for our friend, Devon. That made it somehow bearable. That, and the support from Harry and Jeffrey – and, of course, Fr. Christopher and Sarge.

\*       \*       \*

It was a Wednesday night, about a month and a half into our new 'friendship' with Jake and the boys that we got some information that we were looking for – and some we weren't.

That night Jake had invited us to his place for a party with a few of his close friends and some of the girls that hung around them. I guess you'd call them 'biker chicks'; the girls that wanted to be around those sort of guys and their bikes.

"Hey Harry; why don't you and Wally pick out a couple of girls here that you fancy – hey, it's on me!" Jake laughed as he bellowed this out. He was pretty drunk and in an unusually good mood tonight.

We thought that we'd better use our real names instead of our nicknames since, by some small chance, Jake may have heard Devon use Hap and Slick at some point. We were sure he killed Devon, or had him killed; we just needed proof. He had bragged to us during our brief friendship about times that he had beaten, stabbed, and even shot men in the last few years. But he hadn't mentioned Devon yet. I thought that tonight might be a good time to see if we could get it out of him.

# 42

## The Party's the Thing...

**"It's hard being both the hero and the villain of your own story."**
**-Hap**

"So Jake, this is a great party; the girls are very accommodating and the booze is flowing; but don't you have anything harder?" I said trying to get him to talk first about hard drugs, and then maybe about Devon. It was a long shot, but it was worth a try.

Slick jumped in to help with, "Yeh, got anything we can smoke or snort?"

"Whoa boys! I don't do it any more myself, but I do sell it. I had a bad time with the stuff about 10 years ago. I was doing coke by the pound. It really messed me up. I was young and stupid then. I had a little too much and ended up in the hospital. My folks thought that I was trying to commit suicide. Don't get me wrong, my mom and dad didn't give a shit about me. He was a drunk, a mean one at that; and my mom was turning tricks to feed his and her alcohol habit. Naw, they couldn't care less about me; I was in the way – just out of high school, or should I say just kicked out of high school for banging the cheerleading squad – all of them, ha!"

It began to look like we were about to get the information that we came for so we let him ramble on. Little did we know that what we were about to find out was much more than we bargained for.

"So after a short stay in Buffalo General my dear sweet mom and dad, with the help of the court system had me put away for my own good. Imagine that, locked up with a bunch of nut cases for my own good. That lasted for about six months until I found a way to break out of there and just disappear."

Slick was becoming intrigued by Jake's story and opened up a door we didn't need to look behind with, "What kind of nut cases were in there?"

Jake began to list all of the strange, sad cases he met there until he struck a nerve with us.

"There was this one chick from South Buffalo who tried to off herself; her name was Susie something or other. Anyway, she used her mother's pills to do the job, but her mom found her before they could work their magic. And here's the best part; she said she did it because she was madly in love with some guy. When she told me I just laughed in her face."

Slick and I sat there in complete shock. Was this OUR Susie he was talking about? It was about the right time; the time when she did try to commit suicide. Her mother did find her. She had taken her mother's pills. She did go away to a 'looney bin' as she liked to call it later. This was too much of a coincidence; but I had to be sure.

With a feigned, carefree laugh I asked, "What did this dumb chick look like. I suppose she was short, fat and as ugly as sin." At this I laughed harder and Slick joined in with me.

"No man. As a matter of fact she was HOT. Blonde hair, blue eyes an ass that screamed 'Look at me' – and she knew how to move it, if you know what I mean. And tits…"

"I get the picture, she wasn't bad," I said before Slick blew a gasket and clocked this guy.

I was hoping to move on after this revelation and get to how he did Devon in; but he was just getting warmed up and he wasn't a guy to try to shut up. So Slick and I sat there for the next blow.

"Yeh, she had the hots for this guy named Hap. What a name; sounds like a fag to me; what do you think?"

I was squirming; and what made it worse was Slick's reaction. He busted out laughing and said, "What a name; you're right, it does sound like some fag; ha, ha!"

"She told me that this Hap character and some other chick were getting it on and it drove her over the edge. But I gotta say, what I liked most about her was her killer instinct. She told me she would get that other chick one day. Hey, you know what they say, 'Hell hath no fury…'"

Slick and I were caught by utter surprise. It was like being slapped in the side of the head with a hockey stick. Seeing the look on our faces he thought that we were surprised at his quoting Shakespeare.

He added, "What? I DID go to high school even if I didn't graduate. In fact, I really dug that guy Shakespeare. He knew how to off a guy." Jake laughed as he said this.

It was then that he related to us how he found Devon and killed him.

He continued, "In fact, I used it on a guy just about two or three months ago that needed to be wasted."

Now he was getting to what we were here for.

"About four years after I escaped the loony bin I met up with this guy named Devon; a black guy – and a fag to boot. But I didn't know it at the time, or at least not right away. He rolled into our hang out on Peach Street one night. He seemed cool, so I had a few beers with him and shot some pool. In fact, you two remind me of him. You're not fags, are you?" he said with a laugh, slapping Slick on the back.

Slick and I both stiffened up at this remark. Was he on to why we were there? What would we do if he was?

Not paying attention to our uneasiness he continued with his story, "He could shoot eight ball. The man could run the rack like nobody's business. I made a few bucks off of his skill. He didn't mind; so we hung out there for a while. It was about six months after he started hanging out with us that I found out he was a fag. One of my guys saw him on Chippewa Street holding hands with this white dude. Of course, my boys started to raze me about it; talking shit about me being a fag too. When that started I saw red."

We could see the anger in his face and hear it in his voice as if it were happening all over again, right in front of us.

"That was a Friday night. The next night he shows up there; we had words. Ya know, I kinda liked the guy. He was pretty cool to hang out with and all; but I couldn't have people thinking that I was some kinda fag or something. So when he shows up I popped him. I gotta say, for a fag he could really throw a punch; not no sissy punches, real hard ones. We slugged it out for a few minutes in the bar until I lost my balance and he shoved me through the plate glass window in the front."

He had a look as if we weren't there and he was reliving the fight all over again; blow by blow.

"We rolled around on the sidewalk for a while until I hit my head on the concrete and must of passed out. When I came to he was gone and my guys were standing around me laughing and drinking and exchanging money. They had bet against me, those bastards. It was then that I said I'm gonna kill that son-of- a-bitch!"

We were mesmerized by his description. We could see the anger in his eyes and hear it in his voice as he related all of the details of that night.

Slick sheepishly questioned, "Did you ever get him?"

"You're damn right I did. He has an uncle, an old man, living down the street from the bar; that's where he was staying. After I sobered up and patched up the wound on the back of my head I went down there. At first I rode by every day just looking for him to show his ugly face, but all I saw was the old man. I then had some of my boys do ride bys to see if they could spot him. We figured he wasn't stupid and probably left town that night. So we stopped riding past the old man's place."

I jumped in, "How did you ever find this guy; and where?"

"I didn't find him. Susie did it for me. You remember that chick in the nut house I told you about?"

That hit Slick and me like a ton of bricks.

Finally, after what seemed like a long silence, I asked, "Yeh, but what did she have to do with him?"

"Well it was kind of a round about way that I found him. It was about six years after my run in with that fag, Devon that I ran into one of the guys who worked at the nut house when I was in there. He was one of the orderlies that I got chicks for. I ran into him at the Anchor Bar on Main St. He recognized me and came over to the bar where I was having a beer and some wings. We got to talking over 'old times', if you want to call them that.

Anyway, he remembered that chick and how she and I used to talk together a lot; and asked if I'd seen her lately. I told him I hadn't seen her since when we were both in. He told me that he had heard that she had blown town to go chase the guy she was so hot for. He figured she would probably do that other chick in. I thought that it might be kind of interesting to find out if she did; and it might not be bad to pick up where we left off – so I had him find out what he could about where she went to. It wasn't more than a week later that he called me with the name of the town she was living in. He said he had some friends who were from South Buffalo and knew her sister."

Slick was looking a little nervous by now, but he had to know how much Jake knew about us.

"So where did she live?" Slick asked.

"In Wilmington, North Carolina of all places. Not that far from where you boys live. Isn't that a coincidence?"

Slick was beginning to look a bit nervous at the direction of the conversation. I jumped in here hoping to break the tension.

"So did you get up with her?" I asked.

"Oh yeh. About a week or so after I rolled into town I saw her walking down Market Street near the corner of Third. I was staying in a small motel down Carolina Beach Road at the end of Adam Street. It was a nice day so I figured I'd ride around downtown for a while; it was then that I spotted her. I followed her to her apartment at a place called 'The Carolina Apartments', up about a block or so from where I first saw her. I stayed outside and saw her a few minutes later at a window facing Market; she was on the third floor. She looked like she was talking to someone so I figured I'd wait 'till she was alone. A couple of days later I rode by again and saw her in the window; it looked like she was alone this time, so I went up and knocked on the door. She answered and we talked in the hall for a minute. She was pretty surprised to see me; I would have been too. I told her that I happened to be staying in town for a few weeks and was surprised and delighted when I saw her walking down the street. I asked her if I could come in, but she said she was on her way out to see a friend, a guy named Devon. That hit me in the face. I went there to shack up with a hot babe, but found that I might have hit the jackpot. Don't get me wrong, I would have loved to make it with her, but revenge is a much sweeter reward for me. I wanted to make sure it was the same Devon. So I asked her if that was her boyfriend. She laughed and said no, and that he was a gay black guy – just a good friend of hers. I left, waited around the corner on Fifth Street and then followed her. BINGO! It was the same Devon that I was hunting for; the one I was going to kill. Who would've thought that I would have found him when all I was looking for was to get laid. Ha!"

It was at that point that I knew if I stayed any longer I would've blown our cover. I was fuming; and I could see that Slick was too. In fact, he had two reasons to be hot. But before I could get Slick out of there he pursued the answer that we both wanted, but didn't want to hear out loud.

"So did you get this Devon character?"

"You bet your ass I did. Thanks to my high school English teacher's affinity for Shakespeare I did it with drama. I went to his place one night, knocked on the door and when he opened it I handed him some flowers. What a joke – me playing the role of a fag. I told him that I wasn't angry with him about our little 'tiff' and that he helped me to find out who I really was. I said that I fought him that night because of this internal struggle with my feminine-side bullshit. Anyway, he bought it. The rest was easy."

"What do you mean by that?" I questioned.

"Well, I slipped a 'mickey' in his drink and when his head was whirling I got him full of crack cocaine. Here's the best part, just like in Shakespearean fashion I left my calling card, so to speak. You know, like in his plays he'd have a play within a play, or some shit like that; you know, sort of his trademark. Well I spread out a deck of cards face down, in a semi-circle on the bed next to him. In the middle of the circle I left the king of clubs face up. You get it; 'the King of Clubs', that's me! Pretty poetic don't you think?"

"It sounds like he had it coming to him, messing with you and taking advantage of you in that fight. The bastard deserved dying, ha!" I almost vomited as I said this about my good friend.

Just then Slick had had it. He jumped up and announced, "Man, we gotta go. We got shit to do in a few hours. Hey, Jake; thanks a lot for inviting us to the party. We'll see you tomorrow at the bar, right?"

"You can bet your sweet ass I'll be there. And you'd better be there too. Stay cool."

# 43

## Oh Susie Q

**"I'm on a need to know basis; and there's nothing I need to know."**
**-Slick**

"Well, what did you find out?" were the first words out of Harry's mouth.

"He did it. He gave us all of the details from how he found out where Devon was living, to how he committed the murder," I told Harry and Jeffrey who had been waiting for hours for us to get back.

"Now it's time to go to the police!" Harry announced as he rose from his chair, grabbed his car keys, and led us out the door and down to Precinct 47.

Our sworn statement, even with the recording I made with my micro recorder would've only given the police enough to reopen the case and do their own investigation had it not been for his revealing the evidence of the playing cards that he couldn't have know about. That put him at the scene of the murder. We had done our part; we were out of the loop now. The Wilmington police along with the help of the Buffalo police would handle this.

"You know in all of the confusion and things going on here we forgot about one very important thing," I said to Slick.

"What's that?"

"Susie," I said.

"Oh yeh, I'm gonna have a talk with her about seeing this Jake guy when I wasn't home."

"Slick, you don't get it. Joanie's in danger. Susie told Jake that she would get that girl who took Hap away from her. Don't you remember him saying that?"

"Right; but you don't think she would really do Joanie any harm, do you?"

I reminded him about Joanie's mysterious fall when we were re-enacting my murder mystery at Poplar Grove Plantation, and about some of the strange things that Susie has said recently, and also about Joanie's accident when they went skiing. I told him about how she sidled up to me at their kitchen table just before we left to come to Buffalo.

"I've got to call Joanie and warn her. We left her alone with Susie."

"I hope you're wrong about this, but I wouldn't want anything else to happen to her; she's been through enough already.

# 44

## A Race Against Time

"Death is not the worst thing that could happen to you; everything else is."
-Joanie [from "Where the Road Begins"]
 "But it is final!"
-Hap

It was getting late in the year; fall to be more specific. That was about the same time of year, six years ago, that Devon made his last ride from Buffalo back to his home and family in Wilmington. Slick and I were on our bikes heading down Interstate 79 that goes from Erie to Pittsburg, Pa., stopping every few hours to find a phone to try and reach Joanie to warn her.

It wasn't until we were into Virginia when we stopped outside of Front Royal, trying once again to reach Joanie. She didn't answer the phone so I left another message on the machine. I had a feeling that someone was probably erasing my messages since I was leaving a message telling her that I would call back at such-and-such a time; but she never seemed to be there to answer the next call. If Susie were erasing them then that would mean Joanie was already in serious trouble, if not worse.

"Slick, Joanie once said to me, 'Death is not the worst thing that could happen to you; everything else is. And when she said that I thought that she was right; but death is final! And I could deal with anything that Susie might have done as long as Joanie is still alive."

Slick saw my anguish at not being able to be at Joanie's side, and he said, "Hap; you've got to stop thinking the worst. Maybe she and Susie went on a shopping spree down to Myrtle Beach; or maybe your answering machine is broken. You know that it's a piece of crap, no offense."

"None taken. Maybe you're right for once."

Slick was quick to add, "That's twice – remember?"

"Oh yeh, I forgot." We both laughed at that.

I continued, "I know that she was okay as of a couple of night's ago, just before we found out the details of Devon's murder…"

Slick interrupted, "…and Susie's possible plan, according to Jake, to do Joanie in. Now don't forget you're taking the word of a murderer about this."

"I suppose you're right, again; but I'd feel a whole lot better if Joanie would at least answer the phone once so I could make sure she's alright."

It was then that Slick had one of his brilliant ideas. He said, "Hey, I've got an idea. Why don't I call Susie? You know we've been avoiding calling my place thinking that she was some sort of crazed killer or something. Let me call her and talk to her like everything is fine; and it probably is. Then we can find out if Joanie's okay."

Always thinking the worst, "And what if she doesn't answer your phone or be around to get the next call after listening to your brand new, high-tech answering machine?"

"Easy; we just ride like the wind and get home as soon as we can. You know we can also call Brad or Marie, or some of our other friends and ask them to check on the girls."

"Okay. I don't know what we were thinking. I hate to say it; but we should have thought of this before. I guess we were so caught up in the moment that we forgot the obvious. Let's make those calls, right now."

It was still mid-day so it wasn't unusual that we couldn't get any of our friends on the phone; but we left them messages. It was when Slick called his own apartment that I felt the fear of something bad happening to Joanie come back into my thoughts.

Susie answered the phone.

"Hello."

I could hear her voice through the ear piece of the phone that Slick held to his head as I stood next to him, hoping to hear his answering machine instead.

Caught off guard, and with a quivering voice, Slick responded, "Well, hello. Susie? Are you home?"

"Of course I am; what did you think I'd be doing? I told you last week that I was going to take a few days off of work to take care of some person matters. What are you doing, and where

~ 275 ~

are you? You sound like you're near a highway. Are you on your way home? What are you boys up to? And did you find out anything?"

"Hold on with your questions. I feel like I'm at home watching 'Rocky and Bullwinkle' and you're standing over me hitting we with question after question to try to get me to turn the TV off. No, we're not on a highway, nor on our way home, yet. We're just at an outdoor fast-food place."

"I'm just curious about when you're coming home. I'm beginning to miss you two."

Slick held his hand over the mouthpiece of the phone and said, "Hear that – you two – not me."

He moved his hand and we could hear Susie say, "What was that? I couldn't hear you. Speak up; there's a lot of background noise there. Are you sure you're not on a highway, on your way home?"

I grabbed the phone from Slick; the suspense was killing me.

"Susie, hi it's me – Hap. How are you?"

"Hi Hap. Of course I know it's you, silly. I'm fine. I miss you. Do you miss me?"

I could tell Slick could hear her so I turned away and said, "Look Susie, Slick and I miss you and Joanie, you know – my wife. Speaking of which, have you seen her lately? How is she? I've been trying to reach her all day."

"Well all you had to do was call me." "What are you talking about? Is she okay?"

"Why of course she is; why wouldn't she be? In fact, she's right here with me. She's been staying here for a couple of days now since you boys managed to stay away for months."

"That couldn't be helped. We had to…why am I explaining myself to you? Let me talk to Joanie – PLEASE!"

As I waited for Joanie to come to the phone I thought I heard Susie whisper something into the phone, but it was too faint to know for sure what she was saying, if it was anything at all. It almost sounded like, 'Hap I love you', but I'm probably imagining things.

After a few minutes I heard someone coming back to the phone.

"Hap?"

"Susie? Is that you again? Where's Joanie?"

"Sorry, she's in the shower and said to tell you that she's fine and to call back in a few hours and she'll talk to you. Okay?" "No!

I need to talk to her right now. Tell her to get out of the shower!"

Just then the line went dead!

# 45

## What's that 'Kimosabe'?

*"Men; you can't live without them —but you can sure make their lives
miserable if you try hard enough!"*
-Susie

"Well? What was that all about? Why'd you turn around on
me? You and Susie have something to say that I can't hear? What's
going on? I thought you were my best friend?"

"Slow down Slick. I just turned around because of all of the
noise coming from the passing traffic. She was already suspicious, and
I didn't want her to think that we were on our way home." How I
hate to lie to him; but sometimes it's for the greater good – and this
was one of those times.

"I think that Joanie is in grave danger. When I asked to speak
to her Susie left the phone and came back a minute later and told
me that Joanie was in the shower and that I should call back in a
couple of hours."

"So, what's the problem?"

"Slick, Joanie would never say something like that; not after our being away for so long! And then when I insisted that she go get Joanie to talk to me, the phone went dead. She must've hung up on me!"

"Hap, you might be spinning one of your stories here. You know Susie. It's like she tells me, 'Men; you can't live without them – but you can sure make their lives miserable if you try hard enough!'

"Maybe so; but I'd rather be wrong about this and Joanie be alive and well, than to be dead right!"

"Then let's not waste any more time. We've got a lot of miles to cover before we get back to town."

\*      \*      \*

I hate to say it, but the ride back to Wilmington, despite the stress I felt over Joanie's safety, was breath-taking. The scenery through Virginia and over I-66 and route 17 on the way toward Fredericksburg filled my head with ideas for poems. I don't write very much poetry about nature and this beautiful countryside we take for granted, but I felt a need to do just that.

\*      \*      \*

## The Earth's Bright Green Acres

Surrounded by sites; sounds not made by man,
Inspire the soul; greet the earth, which is grand.

From leaves that hide wonders so small to the eye,
To rivers and mountains that merge with the sky.

It shows us its beauty, which gives us great mirth,
While asking for nothing, but respect for its worth.

The waters flow freely, its gardens abound,
All live together with harmony found.

Beware all those people who don't understand,
What they will not believe in will hurt all the land.

The wasters and careless, but worse are the takers,
Who pillage and spoil the Earth's Bright Green Acres.

\*　　　\*　　　\*

"Hap, Hap, HAP! I've got to stop; NOW!"

"Okay. Sorry Slick, it's hard to hear anything while riding a Harley at 70 mph in traffic flying down an Interstate, but I got it. Let's take the next rest area at mile marker 364. I think it's only a few miles up the road."

~ 280 ~

"Thank God!"

"Well, why are we stopping this time Slick?"

"Hap, you're going to kill us both. It's one thing to be in a car or truck driving for hundreds of miles without stopping, but on a bike it can get a bit uncomfortable. I think I'm getting welts on my ass!"

However angry I might have been at him for making us stop, his comment sent me into a laughing spell. I think it was contagious, because he started as well.

"I'm sorry. I guess it's that O.C.D. you say I have; but I want to get back to Joanie before anything bad happens to her." "You see, it doesn't take a medical degree to diagnose your problem. Even you can see it! And I think you're over- thinking this thing. I'm not blind. I know that Susie still has a thing for you – even after all of these years; and she has always been highly competitive; and her mother was not the best influence when it came to honesty – but I think I know her better than you. I don't think that she would hurt Joanie. I just have that feeling."

"I sure hope you're right. Did you see the last mileage sign back about four or five miles? It said Wilmington was about 60 miles. We're just outside of Warsaw right now. This is the last rest stop before we hit town. So suck it up and get your ass back in the saddle. We're riding!"

"There's one good thing about the welts on my ass."

"What's that 'Kimosabe'?"

"I can't fall asleep while I'm riding; they hurt too much!"

# 46

## And Then There Were Three

**"The shits gonna fly whether it hits you or not. The question is,**
**'How fast can you duck'?"**
**-Sarge**

"Just a minute."

As Susie opened the door we could see by the surprised look on her face that she was not expecting us at all. And we both knew that even Susie couldn't fake a look this good. In fact, I thought that she was going to pass out at first.

"It's just us. We were in the neighborhood, and of course I forgot my key..." Slick began to babble.

Just when we both thought that she would grab him and hug him, she jumped at me and threw her arms around me and began to kiss my neck. I was stunned; and so was Slick.

I think it took only about five seconds for her to catch her mistake and she announced, "Oh Hap, thank you for bringing Slick back safe and sound. You are such a dear friend."

She then turned, letting go of me and grabbed Slick, hugging him and kissing him on the lips.

"Oh, Slick. How I've missed you."

I looked at him, and he looked at me. We were both totally confused by this behavior.

After the initial shock I asked, "Where's Joanie? Is she out of the shower yet?" in a sarcastic tone.

"Don't be silly; that was hours ago. Of course she's out of the shower."

"Well?"

"Well what?" Susie responded acting like she didn't know what I was getting at.

"Well, where is she now? Is she here?"

"No. Of course not; she went back to your place to take care of the plants and do some other things around the house before she left."

"Left?"

Getting a straight answer from her was like pulling teeth out of a tiger.

"Yes, I thought I told you. Didn't I? Well, anyway it doesn't matter."

"Didn't tell me what?" I was beginning to lose what little patience I still possessed.

"Oh, right. She had to go to Raleigh. You remember, now that it's been almost a year her doctor wanted her see a specialist about her leg at Rex Memorial Hospital in Raleigh. I tried to get her to let me drive her there, but she insisted on going alone. You know how independent she is."

"Hap, I think she's right. Didn't Joanie tell you that when you talked to her the other day?" Slick said.

I was now more confused than ever, "I don't know. I remember her talking about Raleigh and some doctors, but I can't remember what she said about them. You know how I half listen sometimes."

"Ain't that the truth," Slick said in a sarcastic tone.

Susie brought us back on track with, "Anyway, she told me she would see the Orthopedist early tomorrow morning and that she'd be back tomorrow before dark. She didn't tell me where she was staying tonight; some hotel or motel near the hospital. I guess we'll just have to wait until she gets back tomorrow night, won't we?"

She quickly changed the subject, "So we can all go out and have a nice dinner, after you both take a shower and put on clean clothes. I'm not letting you take me out looking like that."

Slick and I just looked at each other and then he said, "Who said anything about taking you out?"

"Why Hap did, of course. You'd never think of doing anything so nice for me; now would he Hap?" "I said let's go out to eat?"

Susie did have a way to get whatever she wanted – that is all except for me, of course.

"It'll be nice and cozy – just the three of us!" she said with a devilish smile.

*        *        *

"Slick, I didn't have to stay here. I could have gone home. Joanie might call."

"Hap, you're not making any sense. Why would she call your house – you're not there."

"I know I'm not there! That's because I'm here."

"No, you're not listening – again. You're not there because you're still in Buffalo."

"I am?" I asked.

"Right. To Joanie you're back in Buffalo with me, so why would she call your house when there's no one there? In fact, if she called anywhere it would be here to talk to Susie, get it?"

"Slick, you do have your moments. I guess it would be better if I stayed here tonight. But if she's not home by tomorrow night I'm going out looking for her."

"Hap, if she's not home by tomorrow night I'm going out with you – and so is Susie!"

# 47

## The Missing Link

**"Remember Hap, I don't have stress – I'm a carrier, I give it to others!"**
**-Slick**

"It's going on eight o'clock and Joanie is still not back. I'm about ready to put a gun to Susie's head to get her to talk!"

"Hap, slow down; I told you before I don't think Susie has anything to do with Joanie not being here. Maybe her car broke down, or maybe she got lost. Who knows, maybe she met some good-looking doctor and they're out partying."

"I am going to kill you too!" I ran over to him, brought him down onto the kitchen floor and started to pretend to choke him.

As we were rolling around laughing he said, "Hap, I'm only trying to lighten things up. She's okay. I know it. Something has probably just held her up. That's all. She'll be here; she'll be here. Don't worry so much. You're giving me stress and I'm not supposed to get it. Remember Hap, I don't have stress – I'm a carrier, I give it to others!"

We sat up until two in the morning before Susie announced, "You boys do what you want; I'm going to bed."

Slick and I sat around half playing pinochle for the next two hours until he fell asleep right in his chair. I ended up playing solitaire until dawn. With the both of them out cold I got up, put on my shoes and went out for a walk around the downtown area, wondering what I was going to do.

It was about three hours later that I saw three people in the distance walking toward me and waving. As they got closer I could see that it was Slick, Susie…and Joanie!

I began to run to them as fast as I could. They all just stopped in their tracks and I could see that they were laughing. It was a laughter of joy. I grabbed Joanie as we met on the sidewalk and held her tight, laughing and kissing her as we both held on for dear life.

After a few moments I stopped, caught my breath and looked at her saying, "Where have you been all my life?"

She gave me a coy look and in her best southern accent said, "Why I'll bet you say that to all the girls."

We all went back to our house and had breakfast (I made Slick cook), while Joanie related the ordeal of the past two days.

"The doctors made me stay the extra night at the hospital so that they could see the results of all of the tests before I left. This way it would save me a trip if they needed to see me about something. It made sense; and I didn't expect to see you boys home yet."

"I guess we should've told you, but I couldn't get a hold of you and we thought that, well…according to that guy Jake, Susie was out to get you and we were afraid that she might try to kill you."

When I said this, the girls both began to laugh hysterically.

Slick, trying to sound like 'The Lone Ranger's' sidekick 'Tonto' said, "What you mean WE white man?"

I responded, "Well, you went along with my theory – for a while anyway."

Without skipping a beat he came back with, "Hey, I wasn't the one who developed this whole conspiracy theory, now was I?"

"Alright; I'll take the entire blame for this. But that Jake guy sounded so convincing."

"Hap; when I was in the 'looney bin' I did want to kill Joanie. Sorry dear."

"No problem. There were many times I wanted to kill you too; and Hap and Slick," Joanie said to lighten things up.

Susie continued, "But that was when I wanted to kill myself as well. I'll admit I have had, what I thought, was a crush on you; and I guess at one time I did find you attractive, no offense."

"None taken," I replied just knowing that this was not the end of the insults.

"But over the years, and especially since you and Joanie got married and have seemed so happy together, I've gotten to think of you as my brother; and, God help me, I've really grown to find Slick pretty suave and debonair."

"Is it my imagination or haven't you sort of come on to me – even since Joanie and I have been married?"

"Hap, you have to understand women. No, better yet don't try. I have always been both competitive and a bit of a vixen. It's what my mother ingrained in me; I can't help it. But I've sometimes acted that way simply because it made you so nervous – I thought that that was cute; and it made Slick jealous, which makes him pay more attention to me. But I think I've let out enough trade secrets for now, so I'm gonna shut up."

"You boy will never get it. Hap, that's why I never got too jealous of Susie. I knew why she was doing it; and I knew I could trust you. So, what's the problem?"

"Slick did you understand a word of what they just said?" "No Hap. Did you?"

"No."

"Hap, Slick. Before you do anything else we want to hear what you found out about Devon's death?"

Slick and I gave the girls all of the details about how we found his killer.

Once they were satisfied Slick stood up and said, "What do you say we go into the living room and watch 'Rocky and Bullwinkle'. I think there having a 'Rocky and Bullwinkle Marathon' starting this morning on the cartoon network."

"Great idea; let's go! Ah, girls do you mind?"

~ 289 ~

Joanie just looked at me and sighed, "Of course not; Susie and I would join you but we have to clean up the breakfast mess YOU made. But don't feel bad, given the choice of the two I think Susie and I would much rather do dishes then sit and watch our brains turn to mush. Oh, by the way, the tests came out fine – in case you were wondering. I'm done with doctors, at least for now. But there might be an OB-GYN in the near future."

"Oh good; glad to hear. You know I meant to ask. No, really," I said.

I had forgotten all about the tests she went to take.

Slick, in his classic form, followed her last comment up with, "Why do they always have to spell things? We're all adults."

Then it hit me, "OB-GYN?!"

\*　　　\*　　　\*

### The Future Looks Bright You See

**Living for the moment, with nothing else to be,**
**Learning from the past, is not enough to see.**
**Lying in the present, gives no account of me,**
**Loving makes the more of us**
　　　　　**-the future looks bright you see.**

\*　　　\*　　　\*

~ 290 ~

N.B.: All poems in this book attributed to Hap Pozner, or any other character are the original poems of the author: Michael J. Maccalupo.

# References

Barefoot, Daniel W.; "Seaside Spectres"; John F. Blair, pub.; Winston-Salem, NC; 2002;Brunswick County - "The Cape of Fear"; pp. 17-19 – Theodosia Burr story New Hanover County - "The Fraternity of Death"; pp. 87-89.

Newton-Preik, Brooks; "Haunted Wilmington…and the Cape Fear Coast", A collection of "true" ghost stories; Banks Channel Books; Wilmington, North Carolina; 1995; "The Grieving Ghost of Bald Head Island; pp. 111-116. –Theodosia Burr story.

Zepke, Terrance; "Ghosts and Legends of the Carolina Coasts"; Pineapple Press, Inc.; Sarasota, FL; 2005;"Drunken Jack"; pp. 37-40 – Drunken Jack & Blackbeard story.

"Murder at Ravenswood Hall" is the sequel to "Where the Road Begins" published in 2011.

To learn more about Hap, Slick, Joanie and Susie go back to the beginning of their story, which begins in kindergarten and takes you through their high school graduation. "Where the Road Begins", unlike this novel, is a coming of age story of Hap and his group of close friends.

\*     \*     \*     \*     \*

"Murder at Ravenswood Hall" is Michael's second novel.
His first, "Where the Road Begins", is a coming of age story of a boy and his friends growing up in South Buffalo, NY.
This, his second novel, is a murder mystery that conjures up local legends and myths of long dead souls from the Southeastern North Carolina Coast. Part of the journey to solve one of the murders takes us from Wilmington back to Buffalo. The novel includes original poems written by the author.